PRAISE FOR *INFESTED*

"A thrilling, I-can't-stop-reading page-turner. If *Infested* doesn't make your skin crawl, check your pulse."
—Paul Tremblay, bestselling author of *The Cabin at the End of the World* and *A Head Full of Ghosts*

"Colón is a genuinely gifted writer, highlighted by his believable teenage characters and his ability to move gracefully from grotesque bug infestations to commentary on social and political issues."
—*Rue Morgue* magazine

"Swiftly moving prose peppered with quippy, multilingual dialogue propels debut author Colón's tightly paced paranormal thriller."
—*Publishers Weekly*

"Colón weaves a frightening tale of possession in his young adult debut. . . . Those who appreciate body horror will find plenty to make their skin crawl."
—*Kirkus Reviews*

"Disturbing, hopeful, and exciting, *Infested* is a love letter to the Bronx, New York, that doesn't shy away from the issues that need to be addressed. It's as if Clive Barker's *The Thief of Always* took the 6 train."
—S.A. Cosby, *New York Times* bestselling author of *Razorblade Tears* and *All the Sinners Bleed*

ANGEL LUIS COLÓN

INFESTED

NEW YORK LONDON TORONTO SYDNEY NEW DELHI

An imprint of Simon & Schuster Children's Publishing Division
1230 Avenue of the Americas, New York, New York 10020
First MTV Books paperback edition August 2024
Copyright © 2023 by Viacom International Inc.
Also available in an MTV Books hardcover edition.
All rights reserved, including the right of reproduction in whole or in part in any form.
MTV Entertainment Studios, MTV Books, MTV's *Fear*, and all related titles, logos, and characters are trademarks of Viacom International Inc.
Simon & Schuster: Celebrating 100 Years of Publishing in 2024
For information about special discounts for bulk purchases, please contact Simon & Schuster Special Sales at 1-866-506-1949 or business@simonandschuster.com.
The Simon & Schuster Speakers Bureau can bring authors to your live event. For more information or to book an event contact the Simon & Schuster Speakers Bureau at 1-866-248-3049 or visit our website at www.simonspeakers.com.
Cover illustration by Corey Brickley
Interior designed by Tiara Iandiorio
The text of this book was set in Calisto MT Pro.
Manufactured in the United States of America
2 4 6 8 10 9 7 5 3 1
The Library of Congress has cataloged the hardcover edition as follows:
Names: Colón, Angel Luis, author.
Title: Infested : an MTV fear novel / Angel Luis Colón.
Description: First MTV Books hardcover edition. | New York : MTV Entertainment Books, 2023. | Audience: Ages 14 and Up. | Summary: In a race against time, seventeen-year-old Puerto Rican Manny must rescue his family from a malevolent spirit targeting his apartment building in the Bronx.
Identifiers: LCCN 2022056138 (print) | LCCN 2022056139 (ebook) | ISBN 9781665928410 (hardcover) | ISBN 9781665928434 (ebook)
Subjects: CYAC: Demoniac possession—Fiction. | Apartment houses—Fiction. | Puerto Ricans—Fiction. | Bronx (New York, N.Y.)—Fiction. | Horror stories. | LCGFT: Horror fiction. | Paranormal fiction. | Novels.
Classification: LCC PZ7.1.C644934 In 2023 (print) | LCC PZ7.1.C644934 (ebook) | DDC [Fic]—dc23
LC record available at https://lccn.loc.gov/2022056138
LC ebook record available at https://lccn.loc.gov/2022056139
ISBN 9781665928427 (paperback)

For Marcelo and Amelia—
I hold you both in my heart always

CHAPTER 1

I CAN'T REMEMBER A TIME I HATED MY mother and my stepfather more than the summer before my senior year.

And it wasn't that normal kind of *Oh man, these people don't understand me* bad Disney movie kind of throwback hate. This was mortal-enemy-level hate. It was deep and pitch-black and enough to make me nearly consider getting into death metal.

While I knew I'd change my mind as the emotions scarred over, the laundry list of offenses was too much to bear.

It wasn't enough that she took my car. Not enough that I couldn't see my friends over the summer either—I mean, I didn't have a lot of friends, but still. No, my mother had to choose my very last summer before senior year—the most important year of high school—to hoist an enormous piece of life-shattering news over my head; six little words annihilating all hopes of a decent summer.

"We are moving to the Bronx."

She said it as if she were telling me about what she had for lunch. Like it wasn't a big deal at all, just another enormous change less than eight months after the 7 lb. 4 oz. change that was sleeping in her bassinet next to me showed up. At least I was initially excited about the baby. Did I realize what else came with said baby? No. But at least before she was born, I had the gift of blissful ignorance. This was a straight baseball bat to the face.

And it wasn't like we hadn't moved before. We moved all the time. My stepfather Al's job demanded we did. Since I was ten, we'd moved seven times, and I'd gone to seven different private schools. This, though? The Bronx? Before, we'd only ever moved within San Antonio. And we'd been in our current apartment for eighteen months, and I'd convinced myself that things were finally stable. I'd even made a friend in Clarissa—the only other Puerto Rican in my class. It wasn't like anybody *really* cared that we were Puerto Rican. I mean, most of the time they didn't think we were since we looked white, but it felt nice to know there was at least one other "secret" Puerto Rican like me in class.

But yet another move, and this one across the country?

"Well?" she asked with exasperated motherly expectation. From the look in her eye, that stare filled with embers, each waiting to burst to life, there was only one right answer.

Problem was, I didn't have it for her. I mean, how was I supposed to react? Moving from San Antonio to the Bronx? It was like she wanted my life to be in constant chaos. I only had one year left in high school, and then I'd be out of her hair. A perfect time to go anywhere in the world she wanted with a fresh baby and one less mouth to feed. I mean, come on. The Bronx? Seriously? It felt like she and my stepfather got high and brainstormed ways to make me miserable. I imagined them taking a big old toke and laughing like kindergartners every time they imagined something else to throw my way.

We are moving to the Bronx.

The "we" in that equation did not include me. Before Al, I was totally a part of that "we," but as soon as he entered our lives, everything changed. I got demoted. Al and Mom made me feel like I was lucky to be taken care of, and Al, especially, expected me to be grateful I was allowed to stay in the house. Couldn't they have asked me if I wanted to move? Fine, they had an adult conversation, great, but couldn't they come to me after and let me be a part of the life-changing decision? Couldn't they show me the slightest bit of respect?

My mother used to be my best friend. That changed as soon as she fulfilled her crusade to find me a father—which I never asked for. Then she gave me a sibling, which was something else I never asked for, but I was happier to take the sister than keep the stepfather. Baby Grace was the only reason I liked living with Mom and Al. She was cute, and it felt nice to take care of her.

Mom, though—she changed. It didn't feel like she was quite ready to raise a kid from the start all over again. She pretended she was, sure, but she'd had my grandparents to help raise me. I missed them then. They wouldn't have let her mess with my life this way. They wouldn't have let her take me from home right before my last year of high school to chase whatever new moneymaking scheme my stepfather had lined up, one that was going to blow up in his face because they always blew up in his face. If they were around, I'd have had a place to stay. Wouldn't have mattered if Al, Mom, and Gracie moved to the other side of the world.

"I'm not moving there." I said it with a little bit of a laugh and half a smile, so that I could fall back on it being a joke if she decided to whup my ass. But there was also enough attitude for her to know I was, in fact, serious. It was a delicate equation, and one I thought I'd perfected over the years, if I said so myself. "I can stay with Clarissa, or I can go with David and Belen."

"Ay, Clarissa is barely a friend." My mother arched an eyebrow. "And the Acostas? When was the last time we even spoke to them?"

"They're my godparents."

"They were your father's friends, not mine. And they're nowhere near your school."

I grunted. "Whatever. I'll get my car fixed. It doesn't make sense to leave here so close to graduation."

My mother stared at me blankly. "*Your* car?" And then she smirked. I wished she hadn't smirked. I wished she did anything—anything—to stop me from hating her. But it felt like she was determined, somehow, to keep pushing me further away. "Y quien te hizo a pensar that was going to happen?"

"It's *my* car. *I* pay the insurance on it, and *I* keep up the repairs."

Mom pointed at me. "And *you* are the jodón who crashed it driving around your drunk friends. Or did you forget that?" She sneered. "And you realize that insurance premium is going to go up, don't you? Can you pay for that?"

"I didn't *forget* anything," I said. "I've been applying for jobs so I can handle the extra cost of the car, by the way." I hated talking about the damn accident. Nobody was hurt. Only damage was a dinged-up passenger-side door. Scratched, mostly. Bumper was a wash. Not that any of that mattered; all my mom cared about was that I screwed up. It was a new needle for her to drive into me every time she wanted to dominate the conversation.

"Ay, anyway, on top of all that"—she steamrolled ahead, not deigning to stop and acknowledge what I'd said—"estabas borracho también. Driving under the influence like one of your moron friends."

"I have told you this a hundred times. I wasn't drunk," I said. "I didn't even drink a whole beer. The cops even said I didn't register on the stupid Breathalyzer."

"Oh, I see. So, you're just a careless driver, then? You don't take it seriously enough when you're driving other young people around to not nearly kill yourself and everyone in the car?" Mom was instigating, the way she always did. Questioning and questioning until we argued.

The problem was, I knew which ones to press back on. "I care a lot. Right now, I really care about you and Al dragging me and Gracie from our lives—senior year, my SATs, college applications—to move out to the frigging projects in New York."

Mom huffed, waving a hand as if she were waving away a pest. "We're not going to the projects, muchacho. The Bronx isn't so bad. Besides, your father's getting a big raise and we got family up there, so we'll see more people." She raised both hands in the air. "Sounds like a great deal for all of us."

"Sounds like a great deal for my *step*father. I don't see why I need to move now if I'm leaving next year."

"I'm supposed to give up on free rent in New York?" Mom asked.

Of course, I fell right into her trap. If I let it go, that was her excuse to move on from the conversation as if I'd agreed to it from the start. If I fought back, I was being a brat and didn't deserve the consideration of a voice in this massive change.

"This isn't fair," I said. "I deserved to be a part of the conversation before you decided to make the move."

"Manny, if I can't trust you to drive a car, how can I trust you to stay here all by yourself? How can I trust you to be a part of this decision?"

"The car was a mistake, Ma. And moving for college is different than moving right before senior year. That's disruptive."

"Mistakes or not, you're staying with us. I've got the baby to deal with. I can only do so much, and Al is going to be busy with the new building, so you're going to have to do the bare minimum to repay your mother for living rent-free for so long by helping us however you can."

The guilt was a layered cake at that point. I wanted to fight more. Really make my case. I knew I could finesse the Acostas into letting me stay with them if I had a chance; they'd always felt bad for me after my parents divorced and my dad ran off to Oregon.

Mom shook her head, an end to the conversation, and tossed my backpack to me. She motioned to my room. "Get packing—you leave with Al on Friday in the truck. I'll be there a couple of days later, so you two shouldn't have killed each other by then."

I felt like she'd hit me between the eyes with a hammer.

"And you tell me hours before I have to go? How are we getting there?"

"U-Haul. I bet you'll even get a chance to drive." She smirked. "And it isn't hours; Friday is still three days away."

"Doesn't he have people there to help him who are, like . . . trained to work in a building? Shouldn't we wait until it's ready? What about the baby? Why not hire movers?"

"Manuel Jose, that man has done a lot for you. The least you can do is help him a little before you leave for college. Grace and I are staying here for only a few more days. I need to sort out some leftover business for your grandparents since nobody will be here to do that. In the meantime, you and Al can go ahead and get things ready." She eyed me. "We need to work together. Al's broken his ass to make this happen for all of us."

"Oh yeah. Al's a tremendous help with my mental health. I'm doing awesome, thanks to him."

"Ay, that's right. He didn't help pay your tuition or help pay for the stereo system you had installed in a 2004 Toyota Camry with 140,000 miles. Real monster keeping you in new clothes and letting you concentrate on your studies without bothering you once to get a job." She motioned to my bedroom again with more gusto. "Go and get packed before I get mad, mijo."

In her head, she'd won the argument hours before she even started it. This was her way of simply making her fantasy into reality, and there wasn't a damn thing I could do about it.

CHAPTER 2

A KNUCKLE TO THE SIDE OF MY HEAD WOKE me up.

"Wake up, sleepyhead. We're here." Al cleared his throat before taking a hit from an e-cigarette.

I blinked and rubbed my eyes. The clock on the dash read 6:57 a.m. I sat up and looked out my window. We were parked in front of what I assumed was our new home in the Bronx.

"Did I miss the drive through New Jersey?" I asked.

Al grunted. "Nobody 'misses' New Jersey, kid."

I guess I'd been asleep since Pennsylvania. Al let me drive through most of Texas, but his patience had quickly worn thin since I wouldn't go over sixty-five. That left him driving for the bulk of our time up north unless we had to detour onto a local road—he hated driving local speed limits.

At first I was happy to let him take the wheel, but the boredom nearly killed me. I may not have been a speed demon, but being the passenger, like, 80 percent of the time was mind-numbing. Especially when the roads were dark and surrounded by farmland.

So much fricking farmland.

The houses along the street were packed close and looked weird. A lot of them had more than one entrance at the front. I didn't see many of those back home. Some had more than three mailboxes out front. *How many people fit into these places?* I wondered. No space between people or cars. No sense of privacy. This was the kind of place that nurtured a feeling of irritability, and with only a little more than four hours of sleep, I was super feeling that.

People were already out walking, probably on their way to work. It was strange to see so many people walking instead of driving. Even the people who came out from houses that had a few cars in the driveway kept walking down the street and around the corner.

Alfonso sneezed and grabbed a wad of paper towels from the dash. "Not even a few minutes here and the allergies come kicking in," he said. "Though, at least I look better than you." He cackled into the paper towel as he blew his nose.

That was Al's distinct way of saying "good morning." His distinct way of kicking the groin of the start of my day with no means of climbing back out of the vortex of misery he wanted me stuck inside. He didn't look like the kind of guy who gave off toxic energy. He had kind eyes and wasn't an imposing guy physically. When he and my mom were dating, I even thought he was cool. A little too obsessed with money, but still a semi-decent guy. Decent enough for me to feel like my mom finally made an excellent choice about a man in her life.

Then she got pregnant, and they got married, and in came "Dad" Al. Gone was the cool guy my mom was dating, replaced by a loser who thought every little thing he did was some big life lesson for me. As if he could teach me anything more than what not to wear to be taken seriously by other adults. All his wisdom was condescending nonsense.

I grabbed my phone and checked to see if I had messages from friends.

"Too early to video-call with your girlfriend," Al said with a smirk. "It's six in the morning back in Texas, and she probably doesn't have her face on."

"Her face on?" I rolled my eyes. "Dude, how old are you again?"

"Old enough to know better than to bother a girl at the butt crack of dawn."

I couldn't roll my eyes hard enough.

Before we left, I'd said goodbye to friends, but it all felt so rushed and awkward. There were stiff hugs and lots of promises to FaceTime, but I barely had a moment to digest everything before Al and I were on the road.

"See you soon," my friends had said to me. As if they were sharing a script. Not that I could find anything better to say. They were probably as surprised as I was. I hadn't gotten much time to prepare for the move, and frankly, the idea that I now lived in New York wouldn't register in my brain. I felt like this was a vacation, some time away before the inevitable return home.

That this *was* home—even for a year—felt like a lie. I couldn't accept that.

"Put the phone away," Al said. "We need to get the truck unloaded by noon so I can drop it off. I ain't paying no extra fees. Gas was enough."

"Your gas or the car's gas?"

"Very cute. Move your butt."

I stretched as I got out of the car and took in the building. The facade was all brick and looked surprisingly dingy for a newer building. There were a handful of shrubs lining the front that hadn't grown out yet, with more holes dug for ones that were clearly missing. The smell of fertilizer stung my sinuses. The entryway was all glass, and there was a sign to the left of it that read BLACKROCK GLEN.

"Is that the name of the building?" I asked.

"Yeah. What, you don't like it? It's fancy. Fancy names bring fancy people."

Kindergarten logic. No use fighting.

"Yeah, okay."

Al worked a key off his key ring and held it out to me. "Top floor. Turn the key to the left."

"I know how a key works."

"Do you?"

Whatever. I walked around to the back of the truck to get it open.

"Work fast, Manny. Start with the smaller crap. I'll help you with the furniture as soon as I handle a few things," Al said.

"Sure. Whatever."

I grabbed my backpack and a few of the lighter boxes and headed into Blackrock Glen. The lobby was modern and sleek, with white marble floors and a couple of couches still wrapped in plastic. It looked a lot like some of the buildings we'd lived in back home. There were wires sticking out from some of the outlets, and the overhead lighting hadn't been installed yet—I could see sloppy writing in pencil measuring where holes needed to be cut and wires attached. I got onto the elevator. It had mirrored walls, making an infinite row of my sad reflection holding moving boxes. I wasn't a fan of that. It made me feel self-conscious, as if someone were watching me.

The top floor was dark—only the safety lights were on, giving it a creepy glow. But when I opened the door to our apartment—my home for the next year—I was bathed in sunlight. The floor-to-ceiling windows faced west and north, and I could see the entirety of the neighborhood. There were other buildings visible, some as tall as Blackrock Glen. In the distance, I saw a collection of brown brick buildings clustered together. We'd never lived in a building this tall before, so I'd be lying if I said the view wasn't impressive. I stepped to one window and looked down, watching people walking along the block.

I put the boxes down and did a quick scan of the other rooms. It was clear which bedroom would be mine. Not as big as some of the rooms I'd had back in San Antonio, but not the shoebox some of my friends had warned me I'd end up with. Still, for a luxury top-floor apartment, I'd expected to get a larger bedroom. But outside of the view, the apartment was about the same as our last one. I wasn't sure if I hated this place yet, but it felt like I could. The sterility, the way it almost felt like a purgatory, like it was a place for me to stay a prisoner in until I served the right amount of time—it trumped the views and the marble and the fancy carpets. All bones and no heart. My grandfather always used to say that empty places attracted terrible things. That we needed to keep our hearts full, or darkness would take over. I'd never understood what he meant, but the way the apartment building made me feel made it clear.

On the drive to New York, Al had mentioned Blackrock

Glen had been built less than two years ago and that the original management company completely blew their shot at bringing in tenants. Which meant the building had been sitting more or less empty for a long time—it was understandable why it felt lifeless. The company that Al worked for had swooped in to buy it for pennies, and it was now Al's job to prepare it for tenants. So, maybe over time, things would feel better. Or they'd feel worse. Probably worse.

My phone buzzed in my pocket, and I fished it out. A text from Al. I didn't need to read what it said; I'd been up here long enough to know that he wanted me to move my ass.

I dropped my backpack and raced downstairs before Al got pissed off.

Al was fuming, weaving around boxes as he paced in the now crowded living room. I knew that because he'd gone quiet. It was twelve thirty p.m., and we still had a few more boxes left to unload from the truck, which meant he was now paying overtime on the U-Haul rental. Plus, he'd gotten a parking ticket while we were moving the sofa upstairs.

I could tell that he thought I was to blame, but I wasn't the one who had spent more time on the phone than helping unload the truck. Once we'd finished with the bigger stuff, he had left me to deal with the rest. Every time I came outside to grab another load, I found him either pacing and arguing with contractors or pacing and trying to calm down his bosses (I assumed). If he'd helped with the boxes, we would have been done when he wanted to be.

Al dug into a brown bag and threw a pack of snack cakes on the counter. "I need you to go to the store. I don't think we can get away with this diet when your mom shows up."

"What about the moving truck?" I grabbed a wad of paper towels to wipe the sweat from my neck. "There's still most of Gracie's things to unload."

"I can finish up while you go out."

"With what money?"

Al sighed. "Well, in an ideal world, with *your* money. You're getting older and you should get a job soon. We're living rent-free, but New York's an expensive place, and I'm not going to bankroll your free time once school starts."

I narrowed my eyes. "So . . ."

"So, for the work you help me with, I'll pay you like I would an employee." Al pulled a wad of twenties from his pocket. "Consider this an advance."

I raised my eyebrows. "An advance? Nuh-uh. I know that game. If we need something, I'm happy to get it, but I'm not falling for the front-money con again. You can't throw this on me like that."

Al grunted. I could see the argument brewing in his head, but he simply took a deep breath and said, "At least you're learning." He handed the money to me. "Next time it's out of your pay."

"Can I get us lunch, too?" I asked.

"Finish what we have." He pointed at the snack cakes.

"You just said that shouldn't be our diet."

"Yeah, but that doesn't mean we should waste what we already have. We finish this trash first and then spend money." Al huffed. "Besides, I said we couldn't get away with it with your mother around. She isn't here yet."

I hated the way he walked around my arguments. "Come on, Al. I can't go another day without real food with all this work. I mean it."

Alfonso pouted mockingly. "Poor baby boy can't rough it in the top-floor apartment of this luxury condo?" He laughed and checked his phone while wiping his nose with the back of his free hand—gross. "Get yourself something to eat, then. I'll grab myself something on the way back from dropping the truck off."

"Sounds good."

"I might be a while. After I take the truck back, I'm thinking of heading into Manhattan and showing up at the home office as a surprise. I'm tired, but I don't want these guys to think I'm slacking, you know?"

"Dude, you just got here after driving for a million hours."

Al shook his head. "You gotta hustle, kid."

"Not if it kills you."

Al headed for the door and turned around. "Also, please

do me a favor and get some allergy meds while you're out. I feel like I've sneezed out most of my brains." He motioned around the area. "And when you get home, start unpacking and get as many pieces of furniture back together as you can. I don't want Gracie without a bed, okay?"

Dummy was catching a cold. It was way too late in June for his tree allergies to go kicking in. "Al, the building's really nice and all, but compared to other places we've lived, it looks a little, uh, well . . ." I thought of a million words to say and finally spit out, "Sloppy."

Al rubbed the back of his neck. "We came into this place hot, kid. The guy I'm replacing had a problem with people ghosting him. Most recent was a carpenter, so now I need to find one within the week."

Al's phone rang. He gave me the *Need to get this* face and motioned that he was leaving the apartment.

I found a supermarket three blocks away. It was the longest three blocks of my life. Like literally the blocks here were so much longer than I was used to back home. The supermarket wasn't that bad, though. They had the essentials we needed, and there was a food truck right in front of it selling empanadas, so I killed two birds with one stone. As I ate my lunch, I took in the neighborhood. Everyone seemed so busy, like they had someplace else to be. Back in Texas, things were way more chill—you rarely saw anybody in such a rush. The frantic energy here kind of bothered me, but then I realized I also had plenty of places I'd rather be, so maybe there was something I already had in common with New Yorkers. Besides, it would have been worse if everyone stared at me, wouldn't it? As far as anyone was concerned, I didn't exist, which suited me fine. I didn't need anyone asking me what I was doing there or where I was from.

The thing that really struck me was that there were a lot of Puerto Rican flags around. It was weird to think it wouldn't be Clarissa or my mom as the only other people like me. This place was *very* Puerto Rican. I couldn't help but feel a little excited and nervous about that. I never really felt very Puerto Rican back home, and being in the Bronx wouldn't change that, but maybe I'd make some friends who called empanadas "pastelillos" or understood what arroz con gandules was. I wondered if I could find guayaberas, the shirts my grandpa always wore—I never saw them anywhere in Texas.

I returned to Blackrock Glen—couldn't believe that was the name they gave this undecorated prison—with a few days' worth of groceries and toiletries. That name, though. Like, what the hell even was a glen? I checked on my phone. It was another word for a valley. I thought it was a man's name. The hell did they intend by naming a building after a valley? Was it supposed to be metaphorical? I was amazed. They really paid someone to sit down and use their college education to produce that nonsense. Then again, was that any worse than the other places we'd lived? Most of the condos we'd ended up at had names like hipster hotels: the Alto, the Helix, or the WerX—yeah, with a capital *X*.

When I got back to our apartment, I found that Al had stacked the boxes he'd brought up in the middle of the entranceway, which forced me to put my grocery bags down and move them before I could even get inside. Why did he have to be so annoying? I unpacked the groceries and looked at the mountain of boxes around me. I knew I was meant to start building furniture and emptying boxes. Considering how tired I was of those boxes and of my errands, it seemed like a better idea to tour the vacant building instead.

The top three floors were the same, finished but barren of any details. No light fixtures, only bare bulbs. The walls only painted with primer. Doors had knobs, but many of them didn't have locks, and most of them were missing peepholes or doorbells. Lower down, the rest of the building was in various stages of completion. Some apartments had no doors or any fixtures, and there were entire floors that didn't even have lighting. The carpet wasn't entirely laid in hallways either. There was a lot of work to do—Al and Mom weren't wrong about that. I didn't think I was the guy to help with *all* of it, though. It felt strangely dangerous to live in a place like this. Like everything was half-finished and too delicate to touch.

My phone rang. Clarissa. A FaceTime. I nearly dropped my phone trying to answer it, but didn't want to pick up on the first ring like a loser, so I stopped and let it ring again before accepting the call.

Clarissa's face popped up on my screen. I sat down on the hallway carpet and smiled. It almost felt like I was home again.

"Hey, what's up?" I said, unable to hide the sadness in my voice.

"Hey yourself," Clarissa said. "How's the city?"

I laughed. "I haven't had time to make my mind up yet. We only got in this morning."

Clarissa slid back and turned slightly to face a computer monitor as she spoke to me. "Yeah, I'm sorry I missed your calls. Things were busy over the weekend. I can't remember if I told you I got a job over at the pool." She grinned. "I get to lifeguard, and the only people around are from the swim team, so . . ."

"You're getting paid to sunbathe."

"Exactly how I planned."

"At least one of us is winning."

Clarissa pouted dramatically. "Oh, Manny, come on, don't be so down. You get to live in New York City for free."

"It's the Bronx."

"Is that any different?"

I shrugged. "I don't know. I mean, my mom used to

talk about growing up here like it was hell, but I just walked around a little, and it doesn't seem so bad."

"See! I knew you'd like it," Clarissa said, and then paused to type something. "Are you going to get a job in Manhattan? I'd be so jealous of you if you worked in the Village. I've always wanted to go there."

I shook my head. "Nah, I'm stuck working here for Al."

"Oh, that sucks. You two fighting?"

"Constantly, but it's okay. I'll half-ass my work and screw up enough times to make him fire me."

"Sure you will. You act like you hate him, but you don't."

"You're crazy. Al's the worst."

"He's a corny dad."

"Stepdad."

Clarissa sighed. "Not all of us hate our stepfathers, Manny. How's the neighborhood? Are the buildings super tall?"

"More houses than buildings here. They're packed super tight. But I live on the fourteenth floor, and the view is pretty cool."

"Houses? I thought you were moving into a building."

"Well, yeah, my building is at the end of the block, but there's all houses here."

"I shouldn't act so surprised; it's not like I know anything about it up there."

"Yeah, I was shocked at all the trees, but then I felt stupid. Why wouldn't there be trees?"

"Exactly." Clarissa pointed at me through the screen like a dork. "Challenging our preconceived notions." She shifted in her seat. "You're like a thirty-minute train ride from El Museo del Barrio. You always talked about learning more about Puerto Rico. I bet there's a lot there."

"Really? How'd you know that?"

Clarissa grinned sheepishly. "I might have spent some time Googling for you over the weekend, since I figured you wouldn't think to do it yourself as you just spiraled into your little misery vortex from riding in a truck with Al for a million years."

"Ouch, dude. I don't get *that* miserable."

"Dude, if you could, you'd turn into a Smiths song."

I laughed. She was making me feel a little better. "I did some internet sleuthing myself."

"Let me guess, flight times to get back here?"

"Only for half a day. The rest of the time—"

"Watching movie reviews?"

I sighed. "You know, you're making me happy I'm gone. I did take a few pictures while we were on the road. I was going to send some once the Wi-Fi is set up. Al would kill me if I ate up our data cap. I saw a street sign for Boehner Avenue and figured you'd be a fan of that."

Clari laughed. "Look, I'm sorry to cut it short, but I have some errands. I wanted to catch you and make sure everything was all right. Hang in there, okay? We only have a year left until college."

Exactly. Clari was right. She was always right. "Yeah, yeah, yeah."

"And, Manny, don't get into your head like you always do." She smiled. "It's New York, dude. Go explore! You need to find places to show me when I finally get to visit."

I smiled back. "Yeah, thanks, Clari." I knew Clari could see I was stressed out; she always could. "Seriously. Today's been overwhelming."

"Take it a step at a time, dude," she said. "We'll talk again soon, okay?"

"Got it. And next time I'll tell you about all the places I've been. Promise."

"You better." Clari disconnected.

I felt better . . . until I remembered where I was. Talking to Clari had made me forget my problems for a minute, but reality came crashing down on me. The home I'd known for the last year and a half, the city I'd known my whole life—they were now in the past. A call with Clari was a bit of an oasis, but it didn't change that I was in the Bronx.

I headed back upstairs and stood among the boxes of my old life needing to find their place in a new space.

I wasn't sure if everything would fit, though.

CHAPTER 3

THE NEXT MORNING, AL PACED THE ROOM while holding his phone between his ear and shoulder like a boomer and stopped to slap a piece of paper on the kitchen countertop. I could make out the words "To-Do List" at the top, followed by a bunch of words I knew were going to take a Rosetta stone to translate.

I had slept terribly. It felt like I was in a hotel. Even with most of our furniture in the "right" place—Mom would change everything once she got there—and with my bedroom finished, I didn't feel right. I had the expectation that, at any moment, a slip of paper would appear under our front door with a bill and a cheery message hoping we'd enjoyed our stay here.

I stood in the hallway, staring at the to-do list, and tried to shake the feeling of unfamiliarity.

Al stopped pacing long enough to get a look at me and narrowed his eyes. "Who pissed in your cereal?"

I grunted. "Nobody. Just tired. Didn't sleep well."

Al sniffed. "Yeah, well, don't get too tired. I got a few things for you to take care of." He pointed at the list. "Go on. Nothing crazy. It'll keep your mind off things."

I looked more closely at the scrap of paper and found I could understand some of it. Al had listed apartments and the random little issues in each one he knew I could fix— fun. There was also another trip to the store for me, this time for cleaning supplies.

"But how many more times are you going to allow people to no-show?" Al growled into his phone. He huffed and went back to pacing, each step falling heavier against the floor.

I could tell Al was getting heated, so I decided to get out of the apartment.

"Hey, Al," I whispered, holding up the list.

"Hold on a sec," he said into the phone. "What is it, Manny?"

"What do you mean by 'Fix toilets on ten'?"

"Come on, man. I can't hold your hand through every task."

"Okay, fine. Forget it," I said.

With that, I headed out of the apartment and down to the tenth floor. Al was right—once I got to the first apartment, it was obvious what I needed to do with the toilets. Out of spite, I decided to put some toilet flush handles on backward, and I lost count of how many handles I didn't connect quite right. Al said he was going to pay me, but until I saw an actual paycheck, then he was going to get what he did pay for so far, namely a seventeen-year-old with second-hand contracting experience messing around with a bunch of stuff he shouldn't be messing around with.

As I went about my work, I tried to imagine what I'd be doing if I were still in San Antonio. It was Sunday morning, which meant church, hanging out with Clari at Rivercenter and wishing we could go to the Alamo Drafthouse, and a big family dinner. If it were hot, I'd go to the pool, even though I couldn't swim. I realized this luxury condo didn't have a gym or a pool. It only had me, sitting alone on the bathroom floor of empty apartments.

I wondered if I could even make new friends in the Bronx. I was transferring schools senior year. Literally the last to the party. I'd have no shared memories with these potential new classmates. Was I going to spend the next year with my head down at school and Saturday nights watching animated movies with my mom and sister? Would it be a problem that I was a blanquito—a white boy—in a place that felt much more diverse than where I was coming from? San Antonio wasn't all white, but the neighborhoods and schools my mom kept me in sure were. Maybe I wouldn't fit in here.

After a few hours, I made it to my final apartment on the tenth floor. It was a corner unit with an incredible view. As I entered the bathroom, I flipped on the light switch. There was movement everywhere. Roaches. Creepy, crawly, little shit-brown roaches with twitching antennae and creepy legs. I jumped back and let out a pretty high-octave scream. I looked over my shoulder, worried I might find Al behind me, rolling on the floor in a fit of laughter. The roaches scattered, running off the countertops to the floor and under any gaps they could fit in. There were a handful of brave ones, though, that sat on the fake granite countertops like they owned the damn place.

"So gross," I muttered, looking around the room for something to use to get rid of the remaining little bastards. I had gooseflesh that wouldn't go away—the bugs' movement skeeved me out. As if they were gliding more than walking. The way their antennae twitched back and forth, feeling for something they never touched. The roaches here weren't the kind I'd seen in Texas. These were smaller, about the length of the tip of my pinkie and way thinner. The brave ones seemed to like socializing and were unbothered by my presence.

Still, I couldn't watch them anymore. "Yeah, screw this." I put my tools down and walked out. I decided to see if I could pick up some bug spray on my supply run. I didn't need to be in the same room with those disgusting pests anymore.

CHAPTER 4

I WALKED INTO THE BODEGA ON THE CORNER, hoping it would have what I needed. It was small, and the aisles were super close together, but I instantly liked the shop. It wasn't like the Jefferson Bodega back home, where people flocked for niche snacks and hipster clout. This bodega had things a person actually needed, things they could pick up to make dinner in their own home. This place felt lived in. Marc Anthony—my mom's all-time favorite—was on the radio. There were two cats, both willing to let me give them belly rubs, plus a solid choice of junk food. A whiteboard noted that the place made Cuban sandwiches every other Wednesday but had chopped cheese and buttered rolls available all the time. I'd never had a chopped cheese before. Wondered what that was. If I weren't so full of empanada, I would have asked.

"Uh, hola." I cleared my throat. "¿Tienes, eh, como se dice?" I snapped my fingers. I was slow with my Spanish, and it was hard for me to remember certain words and phrases. "Um, algo para limpiar mi casa?"

The bodega clerk smiled at me. "¿Puertorriqueño?" he asked. "Yo, I speak English, so don't sweat it. What you looking for?"

I felt my cheeks flush. Bad Spanish was something I always got piled on for in San Antonio. "Oh, great. I mean, thanks, man. I was trying to find . . ." I looked at the list Al gave me. "Mistolin?"

The clerk winced. "You need to work on your pronunciation." He pointed toward the back aisles. "It's the aisle to the left right there. We got Fabuloso, too. How much you need?"

Knowing the way Al was, there were things I needed to clean that I didn't know I needed to clean. My best chance was to overcompensate.

"Whatever you got. I need to clean, like, a million toilets and sinks today," I said. That was partially true, depending on how I defined clean versus how others defined clean. My definition was in that realm of dumping enough cleaning product down a drain to make the room smell nice.

The clerk turned and grabbed an empty box before coming out from behind the counter. "You from the new building?"

"Yeah. My stepfather is the building manager."

"Oh. You're Alfonso's son." The clerk frowned slightly.

"Stepson. You met him?"

The clerk nodded. "He was here yesterday getting food. The mouth on him, I coulda sworn he was from here when I first met him. Then he said Texas and I was like, 'I don't see no hat on you.'"

I stared at him. No idea what the hell he meant by "hat."

The clerk mimed putting a hat on his head and spread his stance. "You know, a cowboy hat."

"Oh." I coughed out a pity chuckle. "Yeah, I was never really into that whole look." I pointed at my sneakers. "I'm a little more into Jordans."

The clerk grinned. "I know, I know. I was busting balls."

Oh, cool, okay. Someone else who disliked Al. I could work with that. "Maybe I'll buy him one of those hats for his birthday, then. In case he gets homesick."

The clerk held his hand out as he laughed. "Heriberto."

I shook. "Manny."

Heri waved at my to-do list. "Stepdad got you slaving away, huh? Un pendejo, eh?" He smiled. "My pops was like that too, pero sabes que? You'll be better for it."

I nearly snorted at that one. "I haven't even been here long enough to get my bearings and he's got me on my second errand trip, so yeah, complete pendejo."

"You understand the Spanish," Heriberto said as he walked to the bottles of cleaner lined up on the shelves exactly where he pointed, "but you don't speak. Your moms never taught you?"

"She did, well, a little. I used to speak better when my grandparents were alive, but there's nobody around to really speak to anymore, you know?" I felt ashamed admitting that. It made sense that any skill I couldn't use regularly would fade, but I felt out of my element every time I tried switching to Spanish. Like I was putting on a favorite sweater I wore in middle school: familiar but clearly not in my size. Without my grandparents, the comfort was gone.

"What about school?" Heriberto asked. "Didn't they teach Spanish down in Texas?"

"I took Latin."

"What, you plan on going to Rome? Why not take a language you know?"

I laughed. "It's part of the honors program."

"Like speaking Spanish isn't hard as hell." Heriberto snorted. "Catholic school, right?"

"Yeah, how'd you guess?" I felt a little embarrassed.

"Because only Catholic school is going to act like a dead language is better for you than a language spoken all over the world. They pull the same nonsense up here. My nephew went to Fordham Prep a few miles away. Kid had a choice of languages and took Greek. Not like it's a terrible thing, but I told my sister, his mom, 'Elena, how you gonna let this kid learn someone else's language

when he can't even speak ours?' ¿Es un jodienda, sabe?"
He shook his head and began to put bottles into the box.
"You think you really need everything I got on the shelf?"

"And paper towels if you have them," I said.

"I got some rags I can throw in for free. You need mops?"

"I could use the rags, thanks. I'm good with mops."

"I'll throw one in for free in case, kid. You don't need
that stepfather up your ass, right?"

Man, Heriberto was nice. I honestly hadn't expected it.

"That building of yours," he said. "When they opening?"

"No idea. I think soon."

"Uh-huh . . . You got any idea what kind of people
they're renting to?"

I shrugged. "Whoever can afford to, I guess. I don't know
a lot of the details, but I can ask Al if you want."

Heriberto frowned and waved my suggestion off. "Nah,
it's fine, it's fine. Just a little worried. That place doesn't look
cheap, and from what I've seen, folks who don't live cheap
don't frequent places like mine, you know?"

I was confused. "Yeah, but you're close and you have
things they might need, right?"

Heriberto scoffed. "I got stuff the people already living
here need. What transplants need? Chai? Oat milk? Soy
whatever? I don't got that." Heri laughed joylessly. "Let me
rephrase: I can't *afford* that."

"But if the new people can afford those things, won't you

be able to make more money?" It was an honest question.

"You young and naive, man. They put buildings like that up in Brooklyn and LIC, and they were never intended for the people already living and working in the neighborhood." Heriberto pinched his fingers together and rubbed the tips. "A fancy new building gives the owners of *this* building a lot of justification to start raising rent."

"Oh." I didn't know what else to say.

Heriberto rang me up. "Give me an even forty. I don't have any change right now."

That was good because all I had was forty-two dollars after lunch. Figured I could lie to Al and tell him I paid for the rags and mop.

CHAPTER 5

THE WALK BACK TO THE BUILDING WAS different. I couldn't tell what the problem was, but it felt like the tone of the day had shifted, as if someone had farted but nobody wanted to admit who dealt it. There was something hanging over me. I thought it was from the lack of quality sleep the past few days. It didn't help that I felt completely out of my element, like the earth could swallow me whole at any moment and there wasn't a thing I'd be able to do about it.

I caught a few people my age eyeing me from a stoop as I walked by with my box of cleaning products. I considered giving them a head nod but chose to ignore them. As I waited at a corner for the light to change, one of the guys on the stoop let out a very loud "Yo, blanquito! Hey!" in my direction.

Crap. I hesitated before turning. "Uh, yeah?" I squinted from the sun shining down on me.

"Those real Dunks?" a skinny kid asked.

I looked down at my black Dunks. "I hope so?"

Light laughter.

Awkward silence.

"Nice shoes, then, bro." He sat back down, and then full-belly laughter erupted from his friends. "What size you wear?"

"A ten?" When he didn't say anything else, I turned back around.

A very loud and extended "Diiiiiiiiiiiiick" paired with howling laughter from the other guys followed me across the street.

Having moved as much as I had, you'd think dealing with nonsense like that got easier. But no, I still felt the same mix of fear, anger, and embarrassment. All I wanted was to curl up into a ball and die whenever it happened, no matter how much I knew I should stand up for myself. And what if I did? What would happen if I stopped and told them to go screw themselves? I'd get my butt kicked, that was what. Same as back in San Antonio when I tried to "fit in" with people who were supposed to be like me. I slipped up and got into some-thing physical, and I couldn't even fight. I mean, what was I supposed to say in retaliation? *I know you are, but what am I?*

Lost in those thoughts, I walked back home. Al and Mom had suggested more than once that I be nice, that I introduce myself and let other kids my age know I was new. But that felt awkward as hell. As I approached the building, I stopped short. There was a girl about my age sitting out front in a lawn chair. She had a poster board set up in a halo above her. In large print, it said BLACKROCK GLEN-TRIFICATION.

No lie. That was clever.

She wasn't what made me stop, though. It was the fact that my mother was standing across from her, holding a sleeping Gracie, and very much arguing with said girl, gesticulating wildly at the sign.

"Pero how are you going to do this nonsense without your parents' permission?" My mother was wide-eyed. She had that look in her eyes she got whenever she caught me lying about something.

"Miss, I'm practicing my freedom of speech," the girl replied.

"Sinvergüenza." Mom waved the girl off and turned to see me.

I put my supplies on the ground before Mom rushed over and gave me a massive hug. I gave it back with equal gusto, waking Gracie, who demanded I hold her only to instantly fall back to sleep. It was only a few days since I last saw them, but I hugged them like it had been years. With everything else going on, I'd forgotten how much I missed Mom and Gracie.

"How are you, baby?" she asked as she separated from me and rubbed my back. She fixed my hair. "Ay, you keep trying to pouf up that hair como si tuvieras pelo malo. Thank God you got your grandfather's hair and my complexion." She sniffed. "You smell a little ripe, hijo. When did you last shower?"

I eyed the girl watching us and backed away. "I'm fine, Ma. I'm fine." I ran my hand through my hair to fix the damage and then gave Gracie a quick kiss on the top of her head before handing her back.

"Well, you got perfect timing." She pointed to a Camry parked at the curb, an impatient-looking Uber driver sitting in the front. "Mira, unload the car and come help us unpack. I gotta change this kid's diaper before she wakes up again." She made a face and leaned in. "That poor driver did not have fun stuck in that JFK traffic with your sister wailing."

I smirked. "Well, I wish Al had told me you all were coming. I would have been here waiting for you instead of running errands," I said. "The way he talked about it, I thought you would be here tomorrow."

"Ay, Al's running around like a lunatic trying to get things in order. He's working hard to make everyone who's going to live here happy." Mom gently poked me. "And Mister Uninformed here, you could have texted me to ask when we were coming. It's not like you're disconnected out here." My mother eyed the protester with a sneer.

The protester grimaced back at my mother.

She was right. I hadn't bothered to ask her when she'd be here since I was too busy living in my own head about the move. "You're right, Ma," I said. "At least everything in Gracie's room is ready."

"Bueno." Mom sighed. "I need to go inside." She waved a hand over her face. "This humidity is killing me. I forgot how bad it gets up here. I was hoping we'd have a nicer summer up north."

"Okay, I'll see you up there," I said, making eye contact with the protester as my mother disappeared inside. I picked up my things, nearly dropping the rags on the ground not once but two times.

The protester brightened up. "Hey, you want to sign my petition against this new condo? Having one of the white people barreling into this neighborhood on my list would look pretty good."

"Me?"

"Yeah, you, blanquito."

"I'm Puerto Rican."

She nodded. "Well, yeah, I can see that. You are also white." She held out the petition. "So sign."

I couldn't see what made Mom so angry with the girl. She was protesting, but that was allowed, right? She wasn't yelling or throwing things. If anything, seeing someone my age being friendly was refreshing. Did I love that she saw me as an intruder? Not really. She wasn't being mean about it, though. She sort of had a point.

"Are you okay?" she asked.

I realized I was standing there silent and staring at her. Crap. "Um, sorry . . . I, um . . ."

"Don't be shy," she said with a wry smile. She held out the petition to me.

"Sorry," I mumbled. "I have to clean and um, help my mom." I showed her the contents of the box, as if to prove I wasn't lying.

"Well, before you clean and help your very pleasant mother, maybe you can take a moment to sign this petition." She pointed behind me with her chin. "This building's going to do more harm than good around here, and we need to speak out before it's too late. I'm asking people to sign a petition to get the housing authority to ensure there will be affordable housing in this building."

"Affordable?" I asked.

"Once the trusties and out-of-towners with more money than sense show up, it's over," she said. "They start small. Complain about a smell or a 'safety issue,' and then it all snowballs from there. After that, all the local businesses close. All the local workers get driven out. Then the remaining buildings and houses that *were* affordable magically become unaffordable, and this neighborhood becomes yet another temporary bohemia for a bunch of assholes who are going to move up to Rockland when they have kids for their nannies to take care of."

Between this activist and Heri before, I was getting the

impression that Blackrock Glen wasn't the most popular place. Still, their comments seemed harsh. "I guess," I said, placing my box down. "I mean, not everyone who would move in will be that messed up, though, right?"

"That's true, but like I said, it only takes one or two complaints. I just want to make sure that there's a buffer. That everyone has a chance to live here."

"Well, everyone will have a chance. There's going to be some new people. That might be good for the neighborhood in the long term."

The smirk faded. "Oh, so it's okay for locals to be displaced?" There was a look in her eyes that made my stomach sink.

I shook my head and raised my hands in surrender. "No, I don't mean it like that. I . . ." I sighed. "I'm . . . I guess . . ." Just say it. "I'm not entirely here by choice, but I don't think that's what my parents want."

The look didn't falter. If anything, it got worse. She was judging me. At least I think she was. "But your mom and dad sure seem to be upset about me sitting out here."

"Stepdad," I blurted out before composing myself. "My, um, my stepdad is the manager. We're getting things finished. . . ."

"That's what the 'cleaning' is all about?"

I nodded at my supplies. "Yeah, that's what the cleaning is for."

She snorted and shook her head. "So, you think I'm a problem too? Is that why you were trying to get away from me as fast as you could? Why even bother talking to me, then?"

"Oh, well, you made me feel bad about ignoring you, so I wanted to—"

"Patronize me. Or is it pity because you think I can't handle some random lady speaking Spanish at me like I don't understand it because I'm Afro-Latina and she fails to remember our people come in all colors?"

"Not really, I mean, I don't think what you're doing is wrong, but I also . . ." I tried to think out my next words because, based on the face she made, it was clear nothing I said was landing. "It's like, you know, do petitions really accomplish anything?"

"So now you're telling me that trying to draw attention to this building and what its eventual effect on this community will be is pointless?"

Crap, my mouth and my brain were not working with each other. "No, no, no. Not at all. I mean. I agree with a lot of what you're saying. I don't know if *everyone* moving in here is the enemy." I tried smiling. "I was talking to the guy who owns the bodega up the block. . . ."

"Heriberto? About to get his store shut down because his rent keeps going up every year? The Heriberto who will lose his business the minute one of your tenants gets it in their head that his business is dirty or doesn't sell the right oat milk? That Heriberto?" She crossed her arms.

I felt my mouth open and close. The words weren't finding their way out of me. Change the subject. That was the only way out of the hole I was digging my way deeper into. "I'm sorry, what's your name?"

Blank stare and then a sincere laugh. "Are you trying to get out of this?"

No choice but to be honest. "A little. I mean, look, I wasn't trying to talk down to you or keep an argument going. I'm sorry about that. I'm Manny."

"You're totally trying to weasel out of this, but that's fine." She shook her head and threw her hands in the air. "Sasha. I will be out here *often*, trust me."

Awesome. A single step away from the awkwardness. I couldn't walk away, but I could try to salvage whatever was left of this interaction. Sasha wasn't going anywhere, and I didn't need to have a confrontation with her every day for the rest of summer break.

"Sasha, right. I'm sorry, I really am. I'm not exactly, like, in my element, you know? I got here yesterday morning, my stepfather's being a pain in the ass, and I'm, like"—I tapped my fingers against the sides of my head—"you know?"

Sasha leaned back in her chair and watched me. "Where did you come from?"

"Texas."

"You're not even *from* New York? Your parents, too?"

"Uh, well, I grew up in Texas. My mom's from around here, and Al, well, I think he's from Country Club?"

"Of course he's from Country Club."

"I . . . Is there a reason that should be obvious?" I asked.

Sasha rolled her eyes slightly. "Local thing. Look, Manny. I don't mean to make this weird, but I don't plan on moving from this spot until your stepfather or his bosses address the problems with this building."

I nodded. "You won't hear any complaints from me. I didn't ask to be here."

"But here you are."

There was no winning. I wanted to be mad, but I knew I couldn't be.

"So . . ."

"So." Sasha eyed me and then looked at her petition.

"I can sign that if you want."

"If *you* want, man. I ain't trying to force you to do anything."

I nearly snatched her clipboard, hastily scratching my signature on the sixth line. I made sure to include my address. Sure, I lived in the building she wanted closed, but in less than five minutes, I'd shown enough weakness around Sasha to last a lifetime. I deserved a moment of bravado—maybe. I noticed something on the top of her petition. Her full name, Sasha Betancourt, and underneath, her address—it was the same as Blackrock Glen.

"Hey, wait. I'm sorry. Why is the address here the same as the condo?"

"Because, Manny"—Sasha took the clipboard back and inspected my work, fighting back a smile—"I'm one of your future neighbors."

"Really? But you're protesting the building."

"Just because my parents are forcing me to live here doesn't mean I'm abandoning my values, Manny."

"Oh, right, of course not." I tried to imagine what my mom would do to me if I started protesting this building. "Hey, where do you go to school?"

"Bronx High School of Science. Why?"

"No reason. I need a place to go this fall, so . . ." I hoped she'd say something encouraging, but she stood there looking at me.

After what felt like an eternity, she waved and started walking back to her lawn chair. "Guess I'll be seeing you around, then."

"Guess so," I said, and gave her the most ridiculous thumbs-up I'd ever given another human being in my life. The internal cringe could have made me into a black hole, it was so bad. I used that momentum to grab my cleaning supplies and spin around without waiting to see how she would respond.

I nearly tumbled into the entrance alcove of the building, wincing as the embarrassment washed over me. What was that even? I would have been better off staying quiet and running away, but I had to open my mouth. That girl would stick around, or she'd be back, and every time I saw her, I'd have to remember the mess I made of this first meeting. I couldn't find it in me to imagine the amazing insults or nicknames an imaginative person who was good with poster board could produce the next time we saw each other.

I stood in the main-floor hallway, making sure I was out of sight, and collected myself. Ego wounded, but that was always the case for me, wasn't it? I still actually had to clean.

"Hey, Manny," I heard from outside.

I turned; Sasha was motioning for me to come over. I placed my things down again and walked back outside.

Sasha was casually scrolling on her phone. She looked back at me with an expectant look in her eye.

"That was awkward as hell, wasn't it?" she asked.

I rocked on the soles of my feet. "Yeah, sorry again."

"No, no, no. I'm not looking for an apology. You're the first person my age I've met here, and I assume I'm the first person your age you've met here too. I don't want things to get worse, so . . ."

I stood, waiting for her to finish.

Sasha clicked her teeth and held her hand out. "Give me your phone."

"What? Why?"

Sasha smirked. "Dude, just give me your phone."

CHAPTER 6

"WHY WOULD YOU GIVE THAT TROUBLE-maker your number?" My mom stared a hole through me. She motioned to the stove. "Take your sister's bottle off the heat before she can't drink it." She walked to the fridge. "Ay, nene, I can't understand you sometimes. That girl is threatening your father's work, and you decide to be best friends."

I scoffed. "She's voicing her opinion, Ma, and besides, I need new friends since you guys up and pulled me out of my home to bring me here."

"Such drama. You can call Clari whenever you want."

"It's not drama, Ma. You send me up here with, like, a few days of warning, and now you're mad I'm trying to make friends and not hide in my bedroom for the next year. What should I be doing?"

"You should be helping Al and getting ready for your last year in high school."

"I've been here two days, and the whole time I've been fixing toilets and buying all the paper towels in the Bronx because your husband can't sit down and write me a complete list of what he needs."

"Al is busy, Manny. He needs our help. There's more work than he thought, and I wanted to make sure he could concentrate."

"Well, I'm glad you're here for one of us." That was a smart-ass comment I was going to regret, but I didn't follow up. I wasn't going to apologize for that. I was mad, and with all this change, I had a right to be.

Mom stopped moving and placed a hand on the counter. "You're stressed, so I'm going to let that slide, Manny. It isn't like I don't have things to take care of too. I need to get Gracie set up with daycare, and I need to find out which schools we can register you for in this neighborhood. We're juggling a lot of things."

"I can check on schools. I mean, it would be nice for me to have a choice in that at least."

Mom sighed. "Vete. Go look it up, and we'll make the calls tomorrow. Oh, and don't get cute and email me a bunch of expensive private schools. We're staying public, you hear me? The schools up here are insanely priced, and we don't have the benefit of a scholarship like we did in San Antonio."

Like that really mattered. I was here for one more year. I just wanted to go someplace that didn't look bad on my transcript. That was all.

Sasha mentioned she went to Bronx High School of Science. I Googled it as soon as I got back to my room. It was possible that Sasha lied to me about the name of the school, but there it was. Had a site and everything. Maybe she didn't go there, but that didn't matter to me. The school looked ideal. It had an awesome curriculum. Going to this school would be huge for my transcript. I imagined sending my applications over to my choice colleges and drafting my essay about the struggles of maintaining my grades in the face of such a huge move.

As I navigated to the Student Life section, my laptop screen flickered. Annoying. I wiggled my power cord, and that fixed the problem. I wasn't reading so much as looking to see if the pictures on the site were authentic or if they were stock images bought to make the place look clean or more diverse than it really was.

I was starting to feel surprisingly good about the school, and, knowing my luck, I should have known better: they didn't accept transfers of higher grades. Annoyed, I emailed Mom a link to the school district's website I'd found and left it at that. Wasn't worth stressing myself out about that when I still had work to do.

I went to switch windows back to a Reddit thread on

using all the wonderful cleaning products I'd bought, but my trackpad decided not to cooperate.

"Come on, man," I said as I swiped my finger back and forth, then jammed my thumb down as if that was what was missing from the equation. There was little chance my parents would buy me a new laptop in the middle of a move, so desperation made me a little rougher than I should have been.

Crunch.

It wasn't a mechanical crunch. There was something else to it—reminded me of stepping on an egg. Even after, there was still something that made the trackpad feel off; I couldn't click down on the right side all the way. I pressed down again. The noise was there but less audible, and there was more give this time, as if whatever I'd pressed down had flattened. I picked up the laptop and inspected the bottom—nothing was there. The screen flickered again. This time the left bottom side of the screen didn't recover, the color warping into a muted rainbow smudge.

"Aw, crap, come on," I said as I tapped the screen.

The smudge moved. First along the bottom of the screen, then up toward the left top corner. The smudges then multiplied, all moving around in random patterns. It was chaos. I set the laptop down and tried to soft reset it, but nothing happened. I tried two more times before hard resetting with the power button, though my pressing was met with the same resistance as the keyboard, a loud crunch following the jam of my index finger against it. I felt something wet on my fingertip and pulled it away to see a thin trail of pale-yellow slime spreading from one side of the power button to the edge of the laptop's keyboard. My fingertip was caked in the gunk as well. It looked and felt like warm, grainy snot. Instinct made me wipe my hand against my pants leg, but it still felt dirty. Was there something *in* the laptop? How?

I went back to type in a command prompt, but the keys wouldn't depress right. Some gave in more than others, and when I looked down, I noticed the number pad was moving on its own, as if something beneath was trying to push the buttons up in defiance of me.

Then I saw it: two thin filaments poking from the nine key, extending until a little brown head emerged. A roach. As soon as it made itself known, others did too. From the keys. From the disc drive. From the hinge. Two got on my hand immediately, their legs prickly enough to send chills up my arms and down my back. I pushed the laptop away from me and scrambled onto my feet. What the hell was this? Al said the top floors had been roach bombed, but here the disgusting things were, making themselves a home in my laptop of all places. It seemed impossible that so many could be inside a machine as thin as a laptop, but there they were.

Grossed out, I went to the kitchen to see if we had anything that would kill the roaches. My finger still felt covered in that nasty slime. All we had on hand was kitchen cleaner, but anything was better than nothing. I took the entire roll of paper towels and a small bin from under the sink. I would clean the insects out one by one if I had to. I couldn't lose this laptop, no matter how forever unclean it would be from that moment. I doused a gargantuan wad of paper towel with cleaner and went back to my room with a mission: eradicate the roaches at all costs.

I placed the waste bin at my feet and grabbed the laptop. I gave it a good shake to see if the roaches would fall right into the waste bin. A handful did. I quickly sprayed them with cleaner to keep them from crawling up and out of their prison. After that, I gave the laptop a good wipe down and shook it again. Even more fell out—an alarming number. I repeated the process over and over, each time more little brown roaches pouring out of the hinge of my laptop. I kept looking it over to understand the logic of it. How were there gaps large enough for them to fit through? How were there so many?

I looked down at the waste bin, and it was a quarter full of small, brown roaches covered in kitchen cleaner. It looked like some were dead, but others were slipping against one another and against the soaked walls of the bin. The live ones were scrambling desperately to move up and out of the garbage can. Every time I spotted bugs nearing escape, I sprayed them again. Soon enough, there was a mass of bleach-scented, undulating suds in the bottom of the trash bin. I could hear a low hiss coming from the bubbles. The smell made my eyes sting.

My arms began to ache from holding the laptop up and shaking it, but the roaches kept coming no matter how many times I cleaned the computer. The screen continued to warp and move. The literal shower of roaches now began to miss the waste bin entirely and fall on my house slippers. I kicked those off and kept shaking the laptop. I wasn't going to let the roaches win.

My grip on the laptop had my knuckles blanched white. My shoulders were on fire. I didn't care. I kept shaking and shaking. They could run free through the entire apartment if they wanted; that wasn't my problem. My problem was this goddamn laptop and the little pricks partying inside it.

My anger flared, and I raised the laptop above my head, the desire to whip it down onto the hardwood floor over-whelming. The roaches still fell. Onto my head, down my shoulders and back, down to my feet. I felt covered and finally let go of the laptop. It hit the waste bin, causing the bin to topple over and letting out a tiny tidal wave of soapy roaches across the floor of my bedroom and all over my feet. I yelped and stumbled, nearly falling backward.

The roaches kept crawling all over me, as if they were after me. I brushed them off my arms and chest, but they simply clung to my hands or fell to the floor, immediately renewing their efforts and climbing up my sneakers and legs. I grabbed the cleaning spray and sprayed myself, the cleaner the only thing that seemed to make the vermin let go of me and fall to the floor to die. I stomped the ones that kept moving, desperate to ensure they didn't come back after me.

"The hell are you doing?" Al's voice. Pointed. Annoyed.

Mom followed. "Don't yell at him, Al—pero what the hell, Manny? Why are you wasting all that cleaner?"

I snapped out of my panic and turned around. I was out of breath and sweating. "I was trying to get these roaches—"

"Roaches? Where?" Al stepped into the room and motioned to the floor. "What the hell is this? Jesus, Manny, you're ruining the rug."

"Te dije I wasn't going to deal with that shit if it wasn't sorted out, Alfonso. We got the baby here now," Mom said.

"I know, I know." Al scanned the floor. He crouched down and shook his head at the pile of sudsy, brown roach bodies. "Did you see where they came from?"

I lifted my laptop from the waste bin and shook it. Only a few roaches fell out. "They were in my laptop," I said.

Al stood up. "Did you keep that thing anywhere dirty? Do you think we picked up something from the truck?"

I shook my head. "I had my laptop bag with me the whole drive, and things were fine yesterday." I turned in place, wondering if there were more in the room. Could they be in the lamp? In my bed? "Should we get roach spray or traps?" I wanted *something* that could fix the problem. The idea of sleeping in that room knowing another invasion could happen set all alarms off.

"We can't go spraying that crap with Gracie in the house, and traps never work," Al said.

My mother threw her hands up in the air and left the room. "I need to check the rest of the apartment. For all I know, the baby's room is just as bad."

Al sighed with exasperation. "That asshole told me he got these floors cleaned up." He grabbed his phone. "I don't even know if I can get more money to do more fumigating." He let out a loud sigh. "This place is going to give me a god-damn stroke. Nobody shows up for work, and the ones that do aren't even doing the damn jobs we're paying them to do." He pointed at the roaches. "Clean this up."

I continued looking around the room. I rubbed my fore-arms and chest. It felt like the roaches were still on me.

Al clapped his hands close to my face. "Manny, you still on earth? Clean this up before it stains."

I snapped back to reality and nodded. "Yeah, I got it. I'm just a little freaked out." I looked around the room again. I checked under my shoes. No new roaches.

"You scared of these things?" Al scoffed. "Oh please, the ones up here are babies. The ones down in the basement are worse." He pointed at the floor. "Tomorrow I need you to start with the apartments on nine. The floors still have some paint and adhesive stains. I want them spotless, you hear me? Oh, and fix those toilets from before. You half-assed most of them, and I think it's cute you think I wouldn't notice, but come on, kid, I wasn't born yesterday." And off he went without expecting any answer but my moving to do the work.

I cleared my throat. It felt like I'd swallowed something a little too hot. The cleaner was getting to me. I needed to get a drink of water, but I knew it would be better to power through and clean up my mess. Once I was done, I surveyed my room. No little brown specks. No antennae poking from the molding or knotholes in the faux wood floor. Nothing under my sheets or on my chair. The laptop—even though it stank of chemicals—was fine. Screen worked. Trackpad worked. Nothing wrong. Everything quiet.

But why couldn't I shake the feeling that there were roaches still crawling all over me?

CHAPTER 7

AL WAS RIGHT: THE NINTH FLOOR WAS A complete mess. Whoever handled painting hadn't used tape on the floors, which left me on my hands and knees with a tiny scraper, trying to get rid of weeks-old paint stains from cheap fabricated-wood floor without destroying the staining—a challenge since the stain clung so easily to the scraper. So much for the "luxury" part of this condo. Things felt bolted on over the cheap stuff to trick people. Al wasn't kidding about the lack of money.

"This is bullshit," I said as I started on what felt like the fortieth corner of the living room. I pulled my phone from my pocket and perched it on a windowsill to play a little music. The sound of car horns and random yelling outside wasn't enough to take my mind off what had happened in the apartment. Was I going crazy? It had felt so real. Every little leg scratching at my bare skin. The weight of each roach. The sight of them struggling in soap bubbles, slimy and twitching.

After once again scraping off the finish from the flooring, I picked up my phone and texted Clarissa. Just a "hey" to let her know I was thinking about her. I put my phone back in my pocket and reminded myself it was silly to expect someone to text me back as soon as I texted them. I was the king of leaving people on read.

When my knees began to ache, I took a break from the work and stood up. My mind was going a mile a minute.

"Manny, how's it going?" Al was suddenly behind me.

I nearly swung my scraper at Al, my heart pounding from the start. "Dude."

Al cackled and smacked the back of my head gently. "Easy, big man." He crouched beside me. "How we doing? You putting effort in this time?"

I frowned.

Al sighed. "Relax, Manny. I can see you're working."

"I'm almost done in here," I said. "Two more apartments, and I'm finished with this floor."

Al bit his lip and pointed at a corner I hadn't started yet. "You forget over there?"

I shook my head. "Nope. I haven't gotten there yet. Once I'm done in here, I have to do the bathroom and the bedrooms." Better to say what I hadn't done.

"Okay, then," Al said. "You need anything? I'm going into the city, and I won't be back until later tonight because I need to hassle over some new contracts."

"Nah, I'm good."

With that, Al headed out. My stomach let out a loud growl, and I realized I'd worked through lunch and that it was nearly dinnertime. I felt like getting some air, so I texted Mom to tell her I was popping out and that she didn't need to cook for me.

Heriberto was an expert sandwich maker. His hands moved like dancers, one holding a spatula and the other navigating the little row of cheeses, toppings, and condiments in front of the grill. "You want extra pickles, kid?" he asked.

"The more the better," I said as I leaned against the ice cream fridge and took a sip of Malta. "I'll take a little extra cheese too."

"That's a dollar more."

I arched a brow. "But the pickles are free?"

"I offered the pickles. You asked for the cheese." Heri smiled at me. The man was a damn con artist, but his skill at making sandwiches compensated for this kind of highway robbery. Like, come on, an extra dollar for one more slice of cheese? It wasn't even real cheese. It was a slice of that processed garbage that for some reason tasted heavenly when it melted into a bunch of grilled beef.

The bell on the front door rang, and a few guys my age walked in. They were all dressed in tanks and shorts and soaked in sweat. The biggest guy up front carried a basketball. The group converged on the fridge with sports drinks, and all took turns opening the door and enjoying the frigid air before fighting over who got the last blue Gatorade.

"Heri, dame tres chopped cheese, man." The big guy with the ball stepped up to the counter. I recognized him. He was one of the kids from the stoop.

The kid gave me a look, one I'd seen plenty of times back home. The assessment. He was figuring out who I was and whether I was worth ignoring or bothering. In my few days living in the Bronx, I'd learned that everyone did that to strangers—especially someone who seemed to be an invader like me. The closest a person could get to a friendly greeting was a nod or the occasional "sup." He and his friends reminded me of the football Chads back in Texas. If sports weren't your personality, they couldn't be bothered to try to get to know you. They judged you based on your bench press and nothing else. When I was younger, it made me feel weak and inadequate. Some kids would give in and join the football team, even if they hated it. I couldn't do that. I was a reader. I liked Pokémon cards and going to the movies. The last thing I needed to be was on a team.

These guys? They were all about the "team."

Heriberto already had a row of chopped cheese sandwiches prepped from before and warming near the grill. He grabbed three of the six and bagged them. He then bagged the group's drinks and tossed a few napkins into the bag with a nod. "You winning some cash today, Frankie?"

The big guy, Frankie, smirked. "Nobody's hustling today. Only practicing." Another glance my way, a faint glimmer of recognition. The right side of his mouth lifted a little.

"Please, dude. Ain't like anybody got money out there today," a skinnier guy chimed in. That voice. He was the one who'd asked me about my shoes.

Heriberto spotted Frankie's glance and did exactly what any adult was going to do in that situation: make it worse. "You know Manny?" He pointed my way with his spatula.

I nearly winced at that. An introduction. Awesome. I gave Frankie a nod. "What's up?"

Frankie returned the nod half-heartedly. "What's good?"

"Manny, you play ball?" Heriberto asked, extending the pain of the moment.

"Uh, not really." I shook my head. "Played some base-ball, but I wasn't too good at it."

The rest of the group was staring at me now. Frankie turned. "Baseball" got his attention. "You play for a team?"

"Just my first year. I couldn't keep up with it after."

"Where at, Saint Ray's? Spellman?"

"Oh, um, no. I recently moved up here. I was in San Antonio."

Frankie squinted. "Where's that again?"

"Texas," I said.

A wide smile broke out on his face. "Oh shit, white boy's a cowboy too?"

The cowboy thing was a lot less funny when directed at me. I shook my head. "I've been around a few, but I'm definitely not one of them."

The group stared at me a moment and then broke out into laughter.

"Okay, pardner," Frankie said with an exaggerated drawl. "Sure hope you find some vittles to your liking." He grabbed his things and shook his head as he turned to leave.

The group left, laughing.

Outside, they stopped, and I heard Sasha say, "Oh, shut up, Frankie," before she walked in. She made a beeline to the back after waving to me.

"Great first impression," I said to Heri.

Heri let out a raspberry. "Don't listen to them. They play like they're street. Most of them go to Fordham Prep and never worked a day in their lives. These kids try to use the old Bronx to hype up their reputations, but they wouldn't have survived a day in the eighties. Frankie's the only one of them that's real. I don't even know why he hangs out with them others."

"Were the eighties that bad?" I asked.

"Let me tell you, when I was a kid? If it wasn't on fire,

it was about to fall." Heri cleaned the counter with a wet rag. "Things were wild back then. Plenty of craziness in the world, but man, the Bronx is Shangri-fricking-la now." He pointed to me. "You ever hear of the song 'The Message'?"

I nodded. "Funkmaster Flex, right?"

"Grandmaster Flash." Heriberto looked wounded. "Whatever, anyway, there was a line in that song about broken glass being everywhere, and when I was a kid, that was the truth. The streets used to sparkle. As a man, I realize how messed up that was, but you got so used to it. It was how the Bronx looked."

"My mom always told me it was rough around here, but it seems all right."

"It's still a little rough," Heri said. "But back then more people were in bad shape. No money. All folks had was desperation, and when that happens, people do a lot of stupid things. Drugs, stickups, murders. Cops didn't help as much as make things worse."

Sasha walked back to the counter with an Arizona Iced Tea and a few snack cakes. "Heri, you got Newports?" she asked.

"For your pops, right?" Heri asked incredulously. "You know I can't sell you those. I'm not trying to get a ticket from the city."

"But I'll keep trying," Sasha said.

Heri motioned toward me. "You know Manny?"

"The Prince of Blackrock Glen? We've met." She winked. "I'm messing with you, man. How's the school hunt going?"

"Uh, nowhere," I said.

"Sounds about right."

"I was telling Manny about how the neighborhood used to be," Heri said.

"Bronx was burning if the stories my parents told me are true." Sasha put a ten on the counter. "The old heads play it up, though. It ain't so bad now."

Heri shook his head. "Neither of you woulda lasted ten minutes in my neighborhood." He pointed at Sasha. "Hell, you were born after the last blackout."

Sasha rolled her eyes.

I looked at each of them. "But now that things are better, the people with money realize they can make more money. If they come here, isn't that a good thing?" I asked.

Sasha laughed, collected her change, and walked toward the door. "If I had time, Manny, I'd talk you off that cliff, but Heri's got you. He's the eyewitness."

"See you tomorrow, Sasha," Heri said.

"I hope so." Sasha walked out.

"What's her story?" I asked. "She seems to really hate Blackrock Glen."

Heri smirked. "She's a rebel, man. I don't disagree with her, but I'm sure her parents are ready to kill her with all her protesting."

"Because they're moving into the building she's fighting against?" I asked.

"None of my business and none of yours. Let her do her thing."

I shrugged. "I just can't understand trying to shut down a place meant to house people, you know?"

Heriberto smiled at me. "You need to get past all that naive nonsense, kid, I'm telling you. You're a good kid, smart even, but you need to open your eyes. Being a blanquito keeps you away from a lot of crap folks like me have to deal with, but that ain't no excuse not to learn, you know?" He turned. "Ay coño, almost forgot about your sandwich." He finished up and slid the sandwich across the counter to me.

Some ham looked charred, but I could live with that. I picked it up and took a bite. Salty and savory. I tasted adobo in the meat. It was glorious. Reminded me of my abuela's cooking, for some reason.

"You make the best sandwiches," I said.

Heri smiled. "You lucky I don't charge more."

CHAPTER 8

AS I WALKED HOME, I DECIDED TO CALL Clarissa. Her face appeared and behind her a sea of familiar people. They were at Bryce Miller's house at what looked like a big party. "Yo!" Clarissa smiled brightly. She lifted the phone up to frame more people. "Everybody say hi to Manny."

The group called out my name, and for that moment I almost felt normal. I waved awkwardly. "Sorry to interrupt. Just figured I'd say hi."

Clarissa took a sip from a red cup. "Well, you caught everyone at a perfect time. You wanna say hi to people?"

I did, but I didn't. A rush of embarrassment hit me. They were all having a fun time, and there I was lurking in the dark like a loser. "Oh, um, no, it's cool. I can call again later. I don't want to mess up anyone's fun time."

"Please, Manny. People would be happy to say hi."

"Another time."

Clarissa narrowed her eyes playfully. "Fine. Be shy. I'll call you tomorrow, okay?" She held a finger up, pointing at me. "You can call more often, though. Don't make it one-sided now that you're the big New Yorker."

"It isn't like that."

"Good. Find something to do."

"I will. Bye."

I disconnected.

I headed up to the apartment and found it empty. I checked my phone and had a text from Mom saying she'd taken Grace for a walk. Up here on the fourteenth floor, it was eerily quiet, and I suddenly felt alone. Overwhelmingly alone. Very aware I was alone. I had that weird feeling I got whenever it felt like someone was watching me. I spun around—there was nobody there.

I couldn't shake the feeling, though.

"Nope." I pocketed my phone. I had to keep myself busy. "Chores it is."

I didn't feel like scraping paint, so I grabbed a bunch of paper towels and a mop and took the stairs down to the thirteenth floor to clean bathrooms. Crappy way to kill time, but still a time killer. It wasn't too hard. The cleaning liquids worked well and had a nice scent. By the time I was done with my fifth bathroom, I was sure the world was going to smell like lavender forever.

Two hours later, I'd finished the thirteenth floor and decided to take a rest. I also needed a new mop. I texted Al to ask where they were, and he at once responded with: Basement.

The view from the door leading down into the basement was not reassuring. All darkness. It was like the building's yawning mouth. I reached to the left and right of the door-frame and couldn't find any light-switch panels. I checked inside the stairwell too. Nothing. No light switch at all.

"How do they not have the lights at the entrance?" My voice echoed down the stairs. "Seriously?"

The flashlight on my phone was hot garbage, but it was all I had, so I turned it on. It did next to nothing to light my way and only really helped if I angled the beam toward my feet—which, I mean, yeah, I didn't want to trip over an animal or dead body, but I preferred seeing what was ahead of me too. Every few steps, I swung the light toward the wall. Still no switches. This was insane. How could I navigate down there without light? I didn't want to spend an hour fumbling around in the dark. Hell, I didn't want to spend a second there longer than necessary.

I knew I was being ridiculous. The space was intensely normal. Gray on gray on gray. Nothing out of place. No flickering lightbulbs—that actually would have been an improvement—or broken glass. No graffiti or blood on the walls, as far as I could tell. This was as sanitized as the rest of the building. But something about being underground made it threatening. Maybe it was the idea of all that metal and concrete overhead. Maybe it was knowing I was in a space that felt so much more isolated than being above the street. I wasn't sure. What mattered was it skeeved me out, and that feeling would not let go of my spine with every step I took.

"Why would you put anything down here? Keep things where people won't die looking for them, dude," I muttered to phantom Al. He could've left these things in the entryway upstairs or in front of our apartment door.

Something hit the ground behind me, and I turned. Nothing there. Or at least, what I thought was nothing.

"Hello?" I winced as it came out. Why would I announce myself that way? Wasn't that exactly how the dummies in horror movies got taken out? They shouted out their location for the seven-foot-tall dude in a weird mask and a machete as, like, a courtesy.

Something moved to my left; I spun and shined my light against the wall. Again, nothing. I was jumping at shadows. I needed to find that stupid mop and get upstairs as fast as possible. Easy. Nothing crazy. Once I had the mop, I'd have a weapon, too, which would make me feel a little safer—I hoped.

The sounds in the dark basement were amplified. I heard the faint hum of traffic outside, the air rushing through vents above me, and my own feet on the tiled floor. That feeling of something in the room with me persisted. It wasn't like I was being watched, though—more like something else was taking up space around me. And it shifted. One moment right beside me and the next above me. It left me scared, but not because of any sense that I was in danger. It almost made me feel . . . guilty? As if I was intruding. There was a nagging feeling too. Something familiar. What I'd felt with the laptop. An uneasiness and anxiousness.

Then something ran over my shoe.

I froze. This wasn't a feeling or a moment of delusion. My flashlight was aimed right at the ground, and I absolutely saw something dart right over the front of my sneaker, and what was I going to do now, because it felt very much like something was in that room with me. That original instinct, where I thought I could feel *where* something was, left me. The dark was the threat now, as if it would swallow the pitiful light from my phone and take me away with it forever. Al had mentioned bigger roaches in the basement, hadn't he? That's what it was. Rats made noise, so it wasn't rats.

The supplies had to be close. A few more steps. There was another room ahead that looked like a supply closet. I walked past the threshold and stopped cold when I heard something hissing ahead. A bigger animal? A pipe? Why couldn't I turn around? Did Al have me so screwed up that I would sooner risk my ass than have him bear down on me? If I got out of this basement, I had to have a long talk with my mom.

I reached another doorway and stepped through. I turned in place as I walked in; the vibe was different than only a few feet away. All I saw were the walls—cracked paint made veins across the surface. Old pipes sweating and blistered from the humidity. There were dark streaks all over, as if the dark had fingers and was scratching at the walls, desperate to escape this place. Patches of mold and old filth at the corners. I saw spiders and their webs. Why was this area so different from the rest of the building? Everything else before looked new, but this place felt old. It felt like it had always been there. Maybe the contractors had cut corners. Al mentioned the building was new, but the foundation could have been old. And sure, why not cut corners and leave a murder room attached to your luxury condo?

That hiss came back. This time a lot closer.

"Nope," I said. It was time to turn around. Let Al yell at me all he liked. Every dummy in every movie like this kept walking, and that was when their head got ripped off or the crazy axe murderer chopped off a leg or arm. I wasn't a fan of being axe murdered. I'd take my chances with Al and his stupid jokes. Admitting defeat, I scurried back to where I'd entered, eager to see the light beaming down through the stairwell doorway from the landing on the main floor.

The door was closed.

I knew it was because the light from the lobby wasn't there anymore. My breathing got quicker. My eyes felt hot. I needed to get out. That was the right decision; panicking was the wrong thing to do. There was nobody else here in the building except me and my family. This was silly. And yet I couldn't stop thinking about how Al mentioned that people weren't showing up to work. Why? What had happened to them? Had they gone down into the basement like I had?

Another sound, this time louder, more obviously like feet shuffling against the old tile. I couldn't tell from where, but that wasn't going to keep me from breaking out into a full sprint toward where I hoped the door was. There was a last chance at getting the hell out of this place, and that door was it.

The rush of the run reminded me that I had a frigging phone in my hand—duh—and I went to unlock the screen. My hands fumbled the phone, and it fell, which led to me tripping as I tried to stop short to pick it up. I crashed onto the ground face-first, jerking my hands up to brace my fall.

The jolt of landing made me lose my breath for a moment. My hands scraped against the tiles as I tried to feel for my phone. My fingers brushed aside something with weight. That something pushed back. I yelped and rolled onto my back, slapping at the air. My hands grazed the walls and felt the same thing. Something heavy, moving. Not something. *Some things.*

"You are not supposed to be down here." The voice was raspy and frail. It came from above me.

I tried kicking where I thought the voice came from, but nothing connected. I backpedaled, finding the wall behind me. I looked up, and as my eyes grew accustomed to the dark, I realized the walls and floor had a dull shine. They seemed to breathe.

They were alive with cockroaches.

And they were surrounding me.

"Who are you?" someone else asked. Their voice was stronger.

I struggled to stand, but my legs went dead. The crawling sensation returned, the presence running up and down my arms, brushing the nape of my neck, and trickling down to my tailbone. I was too scared to scream. Pinpricks all over my body from temple to ankle—not painful but enough to overwhelm, enough to feel as if the shadows were trying to grab at me. There was a threat in that feeling, as if the pinpricks could go deeper, as if my skin could pull right off from muscle at a moment's notice.

"Who are you?" This time the question was more insistent. The pinpricks increased their intensity, as if the voice controlled them.

I licked my lips and worked harder than ever to find a breath that could help me say real words. I felt like I was covered in roaches, the weight of them making me feel heavier. I held my breath. This was hopeless. I was buried underneath cockroaches while someone was in the room with me waiting for what? To watch me get eaten alive by these disgusting little creatures? There was a pounding in my head, and my mouth felt so dry. I wanted to lick my lips, but I felt the roaches crawling on my chin and near my nostrils. Felt their legs and antennae poking at me, eager to explore. One hesitantly crawled into my nose, and I couldn't help it. I screamed.

Then I passed out.

CHAPTER 9

MY EYES STRUGGLED TO ADJUST TO THE
lights. I jerked up to a seated position and screamed again,
my breathing instantly heavy. I swatted at my arms and
face . . . but there was nothing there to swat away. I scanned
the floor around me—there wasn't a single roach in sight. I
looked up and scrambled back until I slammed into the concrete wall behind me.

In front of me stood two men, one old and one who looked
to be middle-aged. The younger guy was tall and broad, with
a haircut better suited for someone my age, a severe undercut
that wasn't blended in right at the edges. He wore hipster glasses
and a look on his face that felt threatening. He was clearly
unhappy to see me. Or maybe he had bad indigestion. Either
way, he didn't come off like the most pleasant guy in the world.

"Why are you in this building?" The older man spoke softly. It was one of the voices I'd heard in the dark. This time, I picked up on an accent, but it was as weak as his volume. He looked like he was in his seventies. Messy mop of silver hair. His eyes were a little sunken and had that thing where it looked like he was a single bad word away from breaking into tears. He wore a neat mustache that stretched from one end of his lips to the other. I couldn't get over how thin he was. He wore faded blue coveralls that made it look like he'd drown if he zipped up the front too high. He seemed friendly? Like, I could tell by his demeanor he was trying to make me comfortable.

Didn't help that the old man had a mountain of a dude glaring at me from behind him. That guy wanted me to feel scared.

"You're trespassing," the grumpier younger guy said. The other voice I'd heard in the dark. It didn't have the oomph his appearance would suggest.

I dug into my pocket and pulled my phone out. "I . . . I'll call the cops if you get closer," I said. "I swear to God. I'll scream."

The younger one stepped forward. "You're the one tresp—"

"Lass ihn sprechen," the old man said sharply. He smiled. "Who are you?"

I stared at the men, trying to read whether they were getting ready to lunge at me. I looked at their hands—nothing in them. There didn't seem to be an obvious level of danger, but something still wasn't right about this. Where had they come from? "I'm Al's stepson. The manager here. Of the building." I wasn't about to give my name freely.

The old man raised an eyebrow. "Alfonso Mazza's son? He told me about you. Manuel, yes?" He turned to his partner with a *Did you know about that?* look.

The big guy gave a hint of a shrug.

"I'm Al's *stepson*," I repeated.

The older man held out a hand to help me up. I didn't accept. I wasn't about to trust strangers I bumped into in a dark basement. Instead, I stood up and put a little more space between me and them. I looked around the room to spot the exit. The stairs leading back to the lobby were only a few feet away. I'd been so panicked before, and I'd been so close.

"I did not know Alfonso moved his family here," the old man said with a sigh. "That man does not tell anyone much of anything."

"He's an asshole," the younger one said.

"Peter, rede nicht so," the old man said sharply.

Uh-huh. This was weird. He was right about Al never mentioning things—case in point: a little old man in the building. "Who, um . . . who are you guys?"

"Ah yes. I am Gerhard Mueller." He motioned behind him. "This is my son, Peter."

I nodded. "Okay." I eyed the door. I could run. Get upstairs and call the cops once I was outside. I could see Peter watching me, though. He seemed tense, ready to lunge at me, as if he were hoping I would run. Maybe that was a bad idea.

"If you know my stepfather, are you working for him?" My phone suddenly pinged with a deluge of text messages. They were from my mom, about food and getting dishes cleaned. Very helpful nonsense.

But it was an opportunity, too. I held up my phone and grimaced. "Sorry, my parents."

I texted Al. Who is Mr. Mueller?

New Extemotor. He there?

I assumed he meant "exterminator." That misspelled message took all the snakes out of my stomach. I wasn't completely calmed, but the acknowledgment that this guy wasn't an axe murderer was nice.

Yeah, thx, I texted back.

"Sorry, Mr. Mueller," I said. "Al wanted to know if I found my cleaning supplies."

Mr. Mueller craned his neck to the right and pointed. "There is a bucket and mops in the utility room." He motioned behind him. "There is asbestos and who knows what else in there. Not a safe place for a young man like you." He looked at Peter. "Hol dem Jungen die Vorräte."

Peter turned and lumbered into the other room.

"I'm sorry, is that German?"

Mr. Mueller smiled softly. "Apologies. It is quite easy for me to slip into German with Peter. It is my brain working through both languages."

"Oh, I understand. My mom and grandparents always did that with Spanish. I do it a little, but I don't speak Spanish enough anymore."

Peter returned with two buckets, two mops, and some sponges. He handed them to me with a sneer. "Well, we speak English here."

I didn't think Peter liked me.

Mr. Mueller looked at Peter, one side of his mouth twitching. He cleared his throat. "Speaking more than one language is not a bad thing. You should practice your family's language. It is important to remember your history," he said.

"Um, thanks," I said as I grabbed the equipment. I didn't really know what else to say. I wasn't about to get into my Spanish-language troubles with a German stranger even if he seemed nice enough.

It was funny—for a guy who looked and acted nothing like my grandfather, he radiated the same aura. Familiar. That was the word. Mr. Mueller felt familiar. He felt comfortable. If he hadn't had his leering adult son with him, I would have even felt safe. And I had to remind myself that the two of them had been hovering over me in the dark just moments earlier.

"Will you be okay with taking all of that up the stairs?" Mr. Mueller asked, then motioned to Peter. "My son can assist."

"Yes, I'll be fine." I smiled despite the supplies being a little heavy.

"Good, good. Use your youth." He pointed at himself. "When you get to my age, everything will become more difficult. Everything will be more work." Mr. Mueller patted Peter's shoulder. "It is why this behemoth is good to have by my side."

"Is it only the two of you working the whole building?" I asked.

"Ah yes. It is a family business. Though, if we need assistance, it is simple enough to hire young men like you temporarily." He smiled.

"Do you think it's going to be a big job?"

Mr. Mueller looked confused. Peter sniffed.

"The roaches. Or at least I think that's what you're here for. Is there something worse?"

"There are always vermin," Mr. Mueller said. "Always vermin. Fortunately, there is nothing so bad that I cannot get it out of this building. Your stepfather has made it clear it must be done soon. It appears the last man he hired did not do a good enough job."

That explained so much. Mr. Mueller and Peter were *new* exterminators. Had Al listened to me? That was surprising. I was glad Mr. Mueller would do something about the problem.

"I'm sorry," I said. "But were you both looking for Al?" I still didn't understand why these two guys had been lurking around a dark basement. "I just . . . I'm still a little freaked out, I guess, and being alone in this building . . ."

"Yeah," Peter said, answering nothing.

Mueller glanced at Peter and shook his head. "We were supposed to meet your stepfather, yes, but we heard you and came downstairs, unsure if you were supposed to be here yourself. I suppose this was a case of strange coincidence."

The silence that followed was awkward, and I wanted to fill the dead air. "Well, um, so . . . the roaches. I keep seeing them while I'm cleaning apartments," I said. "The little brown ones. They're the worst."

"Did you know those are the German cockroach?" Mr. Mueller asked. There was a glimmer in his eye. "I always found that amusing. The most common roach in the world, and it is German."

"Is that a bad thing?"

Mueller shook his head. "Oh no, it is a strange thing, but I find pride in it. Something so resilient, so relentless. It shares a homeland with me. That is special in its own way. Unfortunately, it is not my job to simply admire them. It is my job to rid this building of them." He sighed. "It might be hard. These roaches are very virile, strong. They reproduce quickly and efficiently. I hope we do not need to go to the extreme measure of tenting the building, but we will see."

Tenting the building? Whoa. I was sure Al would lose his mind over that. Not a good look if he was trying to rent out apartments ahead of opening and the building was being fumigated.

"Well, thanks for your help," I said. "I should get back to work."

"Yes, do that, Manny. I will see you around."

"Okay." I turned to leave.

"Oh, and Manny?"

"Yes?"

"Please do tell me if you see any other infestation points."

"Oh, uh, sure. Do you have a number I can reach you at?"

Mueller smiled again. "Ah, you will find me easily in this place. We are the only ones here. . . ." He grimaced. "Well, outside of our friends in the wall." He waved and retreated toward the old boiler room.

CHAPTER 10

THE NEXT MORNING, I WOKE UP EARLY—I couldn't sleep after the basement incident—and decided to make myself breakfast. Mom was way ahead of me, though.

"I couldn't sleep," she said as she scooped eggs onto a plate for me. "I ended up unpacking everything." She spun in place to show off her work. There was a pile of flattened boxes in the corner, and everything looked cleaned and placed where it belonged.

"Wow, I'm impressed," I said. I saw a roach crawling near Mom. "Aw crap, Ma, mira. There's a roach next to you." I couldn't stand the idea of getting near the thing, let alone the thought of trying to kill it.

"Ay, pero que jodienda," Mom said as she smacked her

chancla against the floor. "I thought Al said that old man you saw yesterday was handling these disgusting things." She grabbed a piece of paper towel and cleaned the bottom of her slipper. "The baby can't be around roaches," she said, more to herself than to me. "They carry disease. They cause respiratory problems too—I read that the other day. I don't need Gracie getting asthma."

I sat down at the table and took my hand at convincing Gracie that, yes, beige sludge was a totally delicious and suitable thing to eat for breakfast by pretending to eat and enjoy it. The smell was horrific, and she was not buying a bit of my performance. That was fine. Gracie was a good distraction from everything else.

"I'm at the end of my damn rope with these little things." Mom cringed as she inspected the roach guts on the paper towel. "I hope I don't have to clean everything again. I was starting to feel a little more settled here, you know?"

I scoffed. "Yeah, sure, I guess."

"Watch that attitude, nene."

I raised my hands in surrender and gave my attention to the baby. "Sorry, I'm tired."

Al walked into the kitchen and stared at nothing for a minute.

"You okay?" I asked.

"I can't find my keys," Al said softly. His eyes were bloodshot.

"You mean the ones on the carabiner on your belt?" Mom asked.

Al looked down at his belt. "Well, shit."

"You need to go to bed early today," Mom said. "But you also need to talk to the new exterminator. I just killed one of those disgusting little you-know-whats."

Al grumbled, checked his pockets, and left.

"Damn," I said. "Should he be driving like that?"

"He'll be fine." Mom took over feeding duties, and Gracie cooed, excited for the shift change.

"You have more apartments to clean today?" Mom asked.

"Yeah. I got the fifth floor. I'm worried the farther down I go, the more roaches I'll find. The sixth wasn't too hot on the south side. I found a bunch of them chilling in one of the refrigerators."

Mom clicked her teeth. "Well, that old man and his kid better hurry up before they need to fumigate the whole building." She cleaned Gracie's face. "Unless he ghosts Al like the last set of losers. I swear, it's like nobody in this city wants to work."

I shrugged. "You think it's Al's winning personality that's driving them away?"

"Stop, Manny. You know Al's blunt. There's nothing wrong with being honest."

"Fine line between honesty and being an asshole, Ma."

"Language, mijo. The baby can hear you."

"The baby understands nothing I say, right, sweetie?" I leaned in to give Gracie a big kiss and received a giggle in return. "That's why you're my favorite, right? Until you start talking, and then it all changes."

"That's your sister, Manny. You will love her no matter what comes out of her mouth because she is the baby, and when I'm dead, you're going to need to take care of her."

"That's dark, Ma. And hey, what if she needs to take care of me?"

"You're older."

"I know math, but life doesn't care about, uh, seniority or whatever."

My mother scowled. "Stop being a smart-ass. You'll take care of her like I said." She waved me off. "Get out of here and do some work."

I grabbed my phone from the charger. "Are you going to call the school?" I wasn't thrilled to discuss it after finding out Bronx Science didn't accept upperclassmen, but we needed to get registered somewhere.

My mother nodded. "I already got your transcripts over to them. We need to get your medical records, and you'll be all set."

Gracie clapped her hands for more food, which took all of Mom's attention. I used the opportunity to get my stuff together and head out. I decided to take the stairs down for the exercise and nearly ran over Mr. Mueller on the eighth floor. He was carrying more supplies than he should have been.

"Oh, crap, sorry. I'm so sorry." I jogged backward up a few steps.

Mr. Mueller smiled and stood to the side. "You are excused, Manuel. I was also preoccupied. Much to look over, and I am slower than I would like to be." He gripped the stair railing hard enough for his knuckles to blanch.

"I'm slow too, so don't feel too bad," I said. "Oh, hey. Since you're up here, do you think you or your son can check upstairs at our apartment? My mom just killed one in the kitchen, and she's going crazy."

Mueller frowned. "Not good to kill them one by one. They smell the bodies of their fallen. I will send Peter there. Will that be sufficient for her?"

"Oh yeah, it should be fine." I snapped my fingers. "Oh, and I also saw quite a few yesterday on the sixth floor. More than anywhere else so far."

"Are you certain?" Mueller scratched his chin. "I checked there and found nothing. No eggs or dead roaches."

I flashed back to the laptop incident, and my mouth went a little dry. I took a long breath and rubbed my hands. That same cold feeling in my stomach returned. That made me a little angry at myself. Why was I being such a coward? I shook the thoughts off.

"Definitely the sixth floor," I said. "And let me know if

you ever need any help. I don't want to be in your way, but if you or Peter need someone as slow as you, I'm right here."

Mr. Mueller laughed. "Very good, Manuel, very good." He went to go upstairs but turned back to me. "Actually, we do need assistance later today. Will you be busy at three?"

I thought about my errand list. Then again, I'd rather help out this nice old man than my cranky stepfather. "I think so. What do you need?"

"Your stepfather has asked us to look behind some heavier equipment, and while Peter is capable, it would be helpful to have an extra pair of hands." Mueller shrugged. "My eyes and hands are not of much use anymore."

"That's not a problem, Mr. Mueller. I'm happy to help."

Mueller smiled. "Excellent, excellent. I will see you then." He pointed up. "I will send Peter upstairs as soon as I can."

"Great—thanks, Mr. Mueller."

CHAPTER 11

I FINISHED MY ROUNDS FOR THE MORNING faster than I expected. Which left me the big choice: Did I go down to the fourth floor and give Al the surprise of being ahead of schedule? Or did I take a break to get a greasy sandwich and make my first subway trip?

The decision was not difficult.

Sasha was outside protesting our home again. Despite that, I was happy to see her. She was the only person my age I'd met here that I felt normal around. And besides, we were going to live in the same building; it was probably a good idea to be friends.

"Uh, hey?" I waved. "So, you really are going to be here daily, huh?"

Sasha arched an eyebrow. "You seem excited about that.

Were you worried I wasn't going to be around, for some reason?"

I nearly winced from the heat rushing to my cheeks. It wasn't like that. I was trying to be friendly, not flirty. "No, it's not like that. I just meant, like, you said you were going to be here all the time and here you are, you know? It was more of a friendly jokey thing."

"Jokes, uh-huh." Sasha eyed me warily. "Well, if you're going to joke, you need to add a dash of confidence to it, because you might come off like you lack it, but I don't think that's who you are."

An awkward silence.

Sasha leaned forward. "I'm on the verge of pretending I didn't offer that backhanded compliment free of charge, Manny."

"I get it, I get it." I stepped in closer, but not too close. Boundaries, Manny. Clarissa always said I had a habit of standing too close to people. It was how my family spoke to one another. "Look, um, you're, like, one of the only people around my age that I'm on any sort of speaking terms with, and while this is also awkward, I would like it not to be awkward? Does that make sense?"

Sasha held that stare on me again. It felt like a punishment. It went right through me, threatening to dredge out words I didn't want to say. "I mean, if we're sharing feelings, I think it's weird that the stepson of the neighborhood's current biggest bastard wants to be friends with anyone, and if you weren't so anti-smooth, Manny, I'd suspect you were, like, an inside agent."

"I mean, my stepdad only works for the company that owns this place. And honestly, he isn't smart enough to come up with the kind of plan that would make me a double agent, but I could totally be one if I wanted to."

"You find the idea of betraying a neighborhood that is majority marginalized to overprivileged whites funny?"

"That wasn't what I—"

"I'm messing with you again, Manny." Sasha chuckled. "You're easy, man. Everyone in Texas like you?"

I shrugged. "I don't think so; it's a big state."

"Yeah, y'all obsessed with size down there, aren't you?"

"Well, not me."

"Sure you're not."

"You're messing with me again." I felt another flush of heat. Either she was too good at this, or I was making myself a perfect target—it was definitely the latter.

"I am never not messing with you, cowboy." Sasha smiled. "You figure out where you're going to school yet?"

"I think so? My mom said there's a school that's a bus ride down Castle Hill, but I'd rather walk if I can."

"Eh, maybe take you like a half hour? Depends on how fast you walk. You afraid of the bus?"

"Pero que jodienda," my mother said as she came out of

the building holding Gracie. "Why are you like this?"

I turned, expecting to be dressed down for something I'd done. But instead, Ma was making a beeline for Sasha.

"I told you before, if you kept harassing people, I was going to call your parents and the police."

Sasha stood up. "I have a right to protest."

My mother clicked her tongue. "Ay, please. You can take it to AOC. Leave the people here alone."

"It's just you and your family," Sasha said.

"Exactly." Brilliant counter by my mother.

I stood to the side, not wanting to get involved in whatever this was, but I had an urge to tell my mother to mind her own business. Just a flash of the thought. I mean, why was she coming outside to yell at Sasha? It was embarrassing and rude of her.

I took a breath and settled down. No need to be angry, Manny—this was between the two of them.

"Mrs. Mazza, listen, I have a right to lobby my complaints about this condo and its lack of affordable units," Sasha said. "What your husband's employers are doing to this neighborhood is harmful, whether they mean it or not. This isn't going to end well for the people already living here, working day to day to survive."

My mother's eyes widened. "Harmful? Harmful. Este nena. You don't have the first clue about what this neighborhood was like when I was your age. My husband's company is one of the best things that could happen here."

Sasha sighed. "That doesn't mean they make it better by making it unaffordable for the people who already live here."

My mother threw her hands up in the air. "I'm calling your parents. You clearly don't want this building here, so maybe you shouldn't live here either." She went back inside.

"Not to make you mad, but she does have a point. If you're going to live here, why are you fighting it?" I asked.

Sasha began collecting her things. "Local people deserve to live in their neighborhoods, Manny. It's that simple." She slipped her backpack on and straightened up. "I need to get back home and get ahead of the fight with my parents." She shook her head. "No offense, Manny, but your parents sort of suck."

"I can see your point. Though, I mean, I was about to get something to eat. Do you want to walk with me? Or I can walk you to wherever you're going?"

Sasha thought about it and smiled softly. "Fine, I'm down for an Heriberto sandwich. I live in Parkchester right now, so if you don't mind the walk to the train after, since I didn't bring my car . . ."

"No. I like walking. I told you, that was my plan for today."

"Cool, and if you're buying, a quarter water and some Nilla Wafers would be nice to go with the sandwich. I'm high-maintenance like that." Sasha laughed.

I scrunched up my face. "Weird combo. What flavor juice?"

"Red." Sasha side-eyed me. "And why is that a weird combo?"

I shrugged. "I don't know. Sounds like something you'd eat after smoking weed."

"Says the guy with the bloodshot eyes."

I chuckled at her joke. "Red it is," I said. I didn't feel the need to tell her my eyes were red because I hadn't slept well. Truth was, since we'd gotten here, I'd felt off. Like my allergies were about to hit me but wouldn't. Like a pent-up sneeze. Something was there, but it wouldn't come out. And it was only getting worse after the incidents with the laptop and in the basement. I hoped once I got used to living here— and all the stresses that came with the move and opening Al's building subsided—I'd feel better.

Sasha and I walked in silence toward Heriberto's. I had been nervous to bump into Sasha again after our first meeting, so I was glad she was willing to give me a chance to hang out. It wasn't like I was trying to get with her or anything like that. I wanted a friend, and it was nice not to feel as lonely as I did whenever I was in that stupid building.

After lunch, I walked Sasha to her subway stop. I stood at the bottom of the steps leading to the Castle Hill train station and listened to the train roar by above. A crowd of people came rushing down toward us, so I moved aside and watched the wave go by. Sasha simply pushed through the masses.

"Are you okay?" Sasha asked from the top of the stairs.

"Oh, uh, yeah. I just . . ." I was not going to say I was freaked out, but I needed an excuse. "It's a lot."

Sasha made a face. "Sure. I can head off if it's a problem."

"No, no, no. I'm fine, I mean. I'll walk you to the platform."

I made it up the stairs and into the main vestibule where the turnstiles and agent station were located. The heat was somehow worse up there. It smelled like garbage, and the floors were littered with little pieces of plastic and cigarette butts.

Without the crowd, it was silent. There were a few MetroCard machines lined up opposite a booth where someone was supposed to be, but there wasn't a soul there.

Sasha looked around. "I can give you a swipe, or you can jump the turnstile."

"Won't someone catch us?"

"Oh please, this isn't downtown."

Sasha swiped herself through and turned expectantly.

I stayed where I was. "Maybe it's not a great idea."

"Suit yourself, dude. I can stand here for a minute, but I need to go once I hear the train coming."

I nodded. "So, uh, is it cool to ask about that thing from before?"

"That I'm moving into Blackrock Glen and am actively protesting its opening?" ·

"Yeah, that . . ."

"My parents wanted to rent someplace new since they feel like Parkchester's too old-fashioned, and our lease is up. Not like I have much control over where I live as a minor. That said, it doesn't mean I shouldn't fight against something that's benefiting me." Sasha frowned. "Too many people let messed-up things stay in place when those things benefit them. It doesn't seem right."

She had a good point, but I still couldn't wrap my head around it. "What if the building got closed? Where would you live?"

"Dude, it isn't like we're struggling. Like, my parents aren't rich, but they do okay. I wish they weren't so in love with the Bronx sometimes, but it's home." She shrugged. "That said, if we couldn't rent at Blackrock Glen, we'd find something else. I mean, me personally, I feel like it would have been better to just renew our lease or, I don't know, buy an old house. Keep the neighborhood as is, you know?"

"Have you tried convincing them to go someplace else?"

"Not that I wouldn't still fight against that building, but yeah, I've begged them. They say the price is right, and they like the feel of a new building. Not much I can do, you know?"

I heard the rumble of an oncoming train.

"I gotta bounce. I'll text you later, okay?"

"Sure."

Sasha ran up the stairs to the platform above.

I turned and walked toward the exit, stopping in place when I saw an absolute unit of a water bug loitering on the number keypad of one of the MetroCard kiosks.

"Oh, gross, look at you," I muttered.

I was happy that roaches like that weren't as common in our building. Al had mentioned they liked the basements and lower floors, but I hadn't seen any. A win, based on how much more skeeved out the bigger one made me feel. The worst part was, it didn't breathe. If it weren't for the antennae, you'd think it was a toy. Something that big should breathe; something that big should make a sound, let its presence be known before you stumbled onto it and jumped straight to the moon.

I heard another train coming and didn't need a subway car full of people to see some weirdo staring at a roach, so I went back down the stairs.

As I walked home, I took in the sights of the neighborhood. Castle Hill Avenue was totally abuzz, even though it was the middle of the day. There was a restaurant that specialized in Puerto Rican food—I'd never seen that before and decided I'd take Mom there at some point. There were a ton of fast-food places too, but it all felt integrated, like everything belonged together. Back home, you'd have to get in your car if you wanted anything to eat; here, I had, like, fifty options within a ten-minute walk. There was a lot of interesting art around a few corners too. I passed a memorial mural of a guy named Xavier Burton. He looked young. Other art gave love to the Latine cultures in the neighborhood. Puerto Rican, Dominican, and Cuban flags hung from various windows. A dozen different genres of music came blaring out of every other car that passed. I had to admit—it was all cool.

As I was walking over the Cross Bronx Expressway, I got a weird feeling. Like someone was following me and was a little too close. It was the same feeling I used to get as a kid walking home from school by myself. Mom told enough stories of child snatchers that I was always looking over my shoulder, even though we lived less than a quarter mile from my school.

I turned to see that there was nobody remotely near me. There was a group of older women slowly approaching, but that was it. I took a quick look across the street, and all I saw were kids playing on a school playground.

I stood to the side to let the old women pass and waved to them. "Hola, buenos días."

The ladies smiled at me, amused.

I started walking again, my pace fast enough that within a handful of strides, I was about to overtake the women I had let pass me, so I turned at the next corner. I looked at the

GPS app on my phone and saw that I could turn onto White Plains Road and then walk back up Blackrock Avenue from there. I'd be approaching the building from the other side, which was fine.

On that block, the feeling of being followed got more intense, like someone was right next to me. Like I was going to look to the side at any moment and see somebody ready to jump on me. My heart started to race. I broke out into a slow jog and went right into a sprint. I'd like to believe I did it to trick whoever was following me into showing themselves, but that wasn't why. I was scared.

I ran down White Plains, turned onto Blackrock, and kept running uphill. My lungs burned. My legs ached too. I wasn't athletic, but for that eternal ten-minute stretch, I was an Olympian. Not a damn thing in the world was going to get me to stop running. *Move,* my brain commanded. Move and get someplace safe. Get away from whatever it was that brought all this fear into your heart.

And then I tripped—hard. The however many feet of concrete I slid across felt like miles. I quickly sat up, certain that whoever was following me was about to attack.

"Are you okay, Manuel?" Mr. Mueller was suddenly above me.

I almost screamed.

"You were running. Is everything all right?" Mueller looked behind me. "Was someone after you?" He placed his hand on his belt, where he had a small utility knife. There was concern in his voice.

My heart rate was starting to slow. I looked around once more—nothing. I brought my knees to my chest and saw that I had torn my jeans. There were scrapes on the exposed parts of my legs and on my palms. "I'm . . . I'm okay," I finally said. "Just clumsy."

Mueller placed a hand on my shoulder and scooped the other beneath my armpit. His touch was light, as if he was afraid to make full contact with me. He gently pulled, and I took the assist back to my feet. He was surprisingly strong; he had the same secret old-man strength my grandpa had. I felt bad about my assumption of his weakness before. He could probably do the work with or without his son helping.

"You need to be careful in a neighborhood like this," Mueller said. "There are many who would take advantage of your naivete. Weakness is rarely given kindness."

"It's not so bad," I said.

Mueller laughed coldly. "I wish I were still young enough to believe things like that. Come." He motioned to the building. "I have some first aid in my bag. I will help you dress those wounds."

"That's okay, Mr. Mueller."

"You still intend to help me, no?"

"Well, yeah . . ."

"Then we do not need you bleeding all over the apartments. You have done so much work to leave them clean."

Mueller led me toward the building's rear entrance. As the adrenaline wore off and the pain set in, I realized that the feeling of being watched was still there, though it didn't inspire the same frantic urgency as before. Instead, it felt like I was being watched from a distance. I looked over my shoulder and swore I saw something small and dark scamper off down the street ahead.

CHAPTER 12

BACK INSIDE THE BUILDING'S BASEMENT, I cleaned up and bandaged my scrapes while Mueller stood nearby, drinking from an unmarked bottle. It looked like it could be liquor, but I wasn't about to judge. My grandfather said there was a point where a man could do whatever he pleased so long as he wasn't harming anyone but himself. It was a half-progressive belief. I used to tell him he should try not harming anyone, including himself, but he would laugh and say, "I've lived long enough to be content with a few extra bruises"—whatever that meant.

"How are you feeling?" Mueller asked.

"Fine," I said. "My ego is more beat up than my hands. Mom's going to kill me over these pants."

"Why would she care about your pants?"

"I begged her to buy these. They were almost two hundred dollars."

Mueller's eyes widened. "For pants? Your mother spent that much for dungarees?"

"They were a birthday present."

"Very expensive for denim pants. I am surprised they tore so easily."

Peter walked in and snorted. "I could find the same pants for twenty-five dollars at Target."

Rude. "I promise you—these aren't at Target."

Peter kept walking and shook his head.

"I mean, it's more about the brand, not the quality," I said. "You know, like sneakers?"

"Tennis shoes," Mueller said.

"No, sneakers." I lifted a foot to show off my extremely scuffed Jordans. These weren't special, though, so it wasn't a big deal. "Some people pay thousands for these."

"Thousands?" Mueller scoffed. "Why? What do they do?"

"Because they have nothing better to do than waste their money on garbage they don't need." Peter was an expert at lobbing comments while he was milling around pretending to work. It was a weird change from the mute giant of before.

I chose to ignore him. "Nothing. They cover my bare feet."

Mueller blinked. "They do not improve performance in sport?"

"Nope."

"Alleviate pain?"

"I don't know. I don't get pain, I guess."

Mueller stared at my shoes and shook his head. "These things do not seem to be worth the prices you pay for them. Even if you are well-off, it seems ridiculous to me. There is nothing wrong with frugality."

"Exactly," Peter added. "People around here could do well to learn that lesson. If they did, things would be better for them."

That sort of made sense. Score one for grumpy Pete. "I get being careful with money. Al likes to pretend he's good with money. Like, he complained when my mom got them for me. But he never complains if my mom splurges on herself or the baby."

"Perhaps he is imparting knowledge on you," Mueller said.

"Have you met my stepfather?" I laughed.

Mueller nodded in concession. "I do not want to be rude, but my interactions with him have been at times . . ." He looked for a word. "Perhaps it is best I do not speak ill of him. The man is paying for my services."

"Oh, whatever, Mr. Mueller. If he annoys you, feel free to vent to me. I promise you, I'll have a story that's better . . . or worse, really." I picked a piece of asphalt from my palm. That one stung. "I mean, I know Al works hard, but it's easy for him to forget that other people do too."

"A little thoughtless," Mueller said. "But as you told me, the man works for his family. That is respectable."

Respectable. That sounded like a good word for Al. He wasn't an outright villain, right? Mr. Mueller made a lot of sense, and I couldn't help but admire how much he stuck to being calm and polite about everything. I couldn't see myself being so nice if I were working in a big building infested with little bastard roaches that wouldn't go away.

"I think you're right," I said. "Doesn't stop me from getting mad at him."

"Speaking of the guy paying us," Peter interrupted, "we need to get back to work."

Mueller waved his hand at Peter. "Start without me." He looked back at me. "You are young; it is normal to be angry at the adults in your life." He smiled. "I used to argue with my father all the time. He fought me over any decision I made. He nearly shot me when I told him I wanted to come to America."

Peter glowered and walked off.

"When did you come here?" I asked.

Mr. Mueller cleared his throat. "A long time ago," he said. "It was a good decision for me, but not a good one for my father. Still, I had to do what felt right."

"See, I get that. I told my mom and Al I wanted to stay in Texas, but they didn't let me. They forced me here so they could have an extra pair of hands to clean and take care of the baby."

"Did you have any money to stay? A place to call home?"

"No, but I could have figured something out."

Mueller scratched his neck gently. "Any friends?"

"Not really. But only because we moved around a lot, but never like this. We were always in San Antonio, until now. That was easy to deal with. Well, easier." I felt embarrassed talking about it. "I wasn't the best at making friends. Which didn't really bother me until my grandfather passed. He was my best friend."

Mr. Mueller smiled at that. "You know, Manny, there is a difference between wanting your way and needing to do something your way. I took a significant risk—there was no net to catch me if I failed. Our circumstances are different. Your mother may stifle you, but she still provides you with two-hundred-dollar pants. Whether you know it or not, there is a safety net there." He frowned a little. "Two hundred dollars," he muttered under his breath.

He wasn't wrong—in San Antonio, I didn't have any way to support myself. But back home, I knew the area really well, and I was certain I would have been able to find some opportunities to take care of myself. Clari would have helped me get a job if I'd asked. I could have saved up enough to rent my own apartment—it wasn't like the prices were as crazy as they were up in New York. I could have figured it out, but I hadn't even been given the chance to try.

Mr. Mueller stood. "Before you get too lost in thought, how about we take advantage of the time you have volunteered to assist us?" He took a deep breath. "Come along. Peter and I could use your help upstairs."

I checked my bandages. I was good to go. Pants weren't too bad, but I wasn't looking forward to telling my mom what happened. Mr. Mueller was right. I could always worry about what I was going to do about that later.

CHAPTER 13

WE FOUND A NEST ON THE ELEVENTH floor, just three floors below where my apartment was. Hundreds of the little brown monsters. They crawled over each other in a panic when Mr. Mueller shined his Maglite on them. Even with so many of them huddled into a corner, their legs didn't make a sound. They darted back and forth, making for the little seams between the wall and baseboard molding. I kept my distance, hovering behind Mr. Mueller, unable to step forward for fear the roaches would come at me.

"Do we spray them?" I regretted offering to help Mr. Mueller in the building instead of helping Peter with their equipment outside. Then again, Peter really didn't seem to want me around him.

Mr. Mueller shook his head. "No. This apartment needs to be fumigated. Maybe even this floor." He frowned. "I do not think it is safe for your mother and a baby to be in this building."

I sighed. "And Al wants to get renters in here next month."

"That is in two weeks."

"I know."

Mr. Mueller stepped away from the roach party, puffed out his cheeks, and crossed his arms. "Your stepfather is going to be disappointed. I do not believe this building is ready at all."

"Didn't he already have this place fumigated?"

"Did he?"

"That's what he told me."

"Ah, well, whoever Alfonso dealt with was a liar at best and a thief at worst. They did not do a thorough job." He motioned to a roach crawling on a countertop. "Roaches may not seem intelligent, but this brazenness is not the act of an animal that was recently assaulted."

I nearly laughed at the way Mueller talked about the roach. Like it was a lion or something. "You think they remember?"

"Everything remembers, Manuel. Trauma is a great motivator of memory. Without that, there is no survival, and these creatures are efficient survivors."

"They can survive a nuke, right?"

"Survived," Mueller said. "I am more than confident there are relatives of our little friends here living happily in Chernobyl. It is admirable. Their resilience in the face of those who would do anything to exterminate them. Very relatable."

That was a little weird. Sure, they survived crazy things, but they were filthy and creepy. I didn't care how resilient the roaches were—there had to be a way to get them out of this building. Let them be admired from afar, not from my bedroom.

"Do you think they're coming from somewhere else?" I asked.

Mueller thought about that as he checked other cabinets. "Even more in here," he muttered. "I do not know if they come from another home on this block. There are one or two abandoned ones. But I doubt it. These creatures only live for a hundred days. There is not much time for migration. They stay where they thrive and will slowly move elsewhere when there is opportunity."

"That's how they came here from Germany, right?"

Mueller scoffed. "They may be the German roach, but they could be from anywhere. These are the most common in the world. I would imagine there are trillions and trillions of them."

I imagined what that looked like, and my mind couldn't

handle the scale. Trillions. All those legs and brown carapaces. I wondered if that quantity of them would finally
make a noise. Would their weight collapse anything they
nested in? I remembered the weight of them on my body in
the basement and shuddered. But they were so small; it was
easy to imagine a trillion of these crawling through the sewers beneath the city. Maybe even more than that. Was a qua-
drillion feasible? Could I even imagine a number that high?

"There are dozens of eggs here too," Mueller said. "This
cannot be resolved with traps or some spray." He stood up
from his crouch. "I will need to discuss this with Alfonso in
the morning. He may not be happy about this news, but this
must be done the right way."

"Should we be living here?"

"I would not recommend it, but that is for your stepfather to decide."

That worried me. Not because Al would make the wrong
decision—I knew he would protect Gracie—but I was certain
he would be in the absolute worst mood. Those moods had
a habit of turning their head to me, and I sucked at confrontation. Even when I tried standing up for myself, Al always
steamrolled over me.

"Do you want me to tell him?" I asked.

Mueller waved my suggestion off. "No, no. I do not want
him to get angry with you. This is not your fault."

"I mean, it isn't yours, either, Mr. Mueller. It's nature, right?"

"I suppose that is right, but Alfonso hired me to assess this problem and provide my input. He can choose to ignore me and open the building if needed. That will be up to him and his employers."

"Well, at least he'll be glad that he found some dependable people to do the job. I'm happy to help too if you both need a hand."

Mueller made a face and moved on. "I do appreciate that. You will be able to assist me with examining the other floors. I hope that we will only need to treat this floor and not the entire building."

"What happens if they need to do the entire building?"

Mueller scratched the back of his head. "It will need to be closed. Those chemicals are dangerous. And then we will need to clean and assess whether the infestation has been resolved. These things are not exact, and as I said, roaches are a resilient species. We have yet to find a definitive way of eliminating them entirely. It may work for now, yet they will still return." He raised a finger. "It only takes one survivor to bring the problem back all over again."

If Mueller was right, there was no way Al was going to meet his deadline. And if he didn't, what then? Would Al be in trouble? Would we be out of a home in one of the most expensive cities in the country? It wasn't as if I cared if Al was happy or anything, but I didn't want to see him outright fail. Then again, he'd set us up for this, hadn't he? He could have come here alone and checked it out before he dragged his family into this situation. Al didn't need to rush into this job and move mountains just for free rent and a change of scenery. If anything, his selfishness was at fault here.

The building was a curse he'd brought on himself, and my family was being saddled with it too.

The worry set in bad then. I absent-mindedly placed my left hand on the counter and pulled it back when pain shot up my palm. It stung at first, but then the pain amplified. An immense amount of pressure ran from the heel of my hand up my wrist and into my elbow. I hissed my next breath and held my hand in the other.

"Ow, shit. What the hell?"

"Are you okay?" Mueller was walking to the apartment's door.

"Oh, uh, yeah. I must have hit my hand harder than I thought. I'll be right back." I rushed over to the bathroom, the pain worsening. My hand felt three times its normal size. Every finger throbbed. What the hell was wrong with it?

I closed the door to the bathroom behind me and ran the sink. I tore the Band-Aid off my hand—there was fresh blood. The scrape that ran from the bottom of my hand to the base of my thumb was wet and slick as if the wound had opened back up. I stuck my hand under the water and winced as the pain grew. It felt as if my thumb was about to fall off any second. As if the bone was beginning to crack.

Had I broken something? But why would the response be so delayed?

I brushed the scrape gently with the fingers of my free hand. It looked the same as before—just some scraped skin. Nothing out of the ordinary. I cut the water off and used a wad of toilet paper to dry my hand. As I applied pressure, I felt a huge jolt of pain from under my skin . . . like something was pushing back.

Or trying to get out.

I pulled the toilet paper away and brought my hand closer to my face. The skin on my palm was moving. There was something under there. The pain was excruciating and getting worse by the second. I caught whatever it was between my fingers and squeezed as hard as I could. I could pinch them out, like a zit, I thought. Something writhed between my fingers, as if it were trying to pull away. I squeezed harder and harder, until I felt my skin split. Blood began to trickle down my wrist. And then I saw something poke out from between my fingers—two thin strands, both moving independently.

Antennae.

A head emerged, then a pill-shaped brown body, covered in blood. I flicked my wrist and yelped. The roach and blood landed on the mirrored medicine cabinet in front of me. I looked at my bleeding hand—the skin was still moving. There were more of them in there. I squeezed again, hard as I could. Another came out, and then another and another. Some of them were still alive and raced around the sink where they'd fallen. Others came out split or crushed, the greenish yellow of their insides oozing out of the wound and mixing with my blood. Now that the skin was split, it felt like the flow of roaches wouldn't end, like the pain would go on forever. I was filled with them. I looked up and thought I saw Mr. Mueller behind me in the reflection of the bathroom mirror. I spun on my heel.

There was nobody there.

I screamed and kept squeezing at my wound. I had to get them out. Every single roach. I slammed my hand against the sink, hoping the blows would crush the bugs and make the steady stream of vermin stop. But it didn't help; they kept coming and coming. I held my hand up and watched them twitch and writhe. An anger welled up inside me, something I hadn't felt before. An animal anger, no reason, no logic. This place was what did this to me. This horrible, horrible building. The move. Al and Mom making these decisions for me. If it weren't for Blackrock Glen, everything would be better.

I roared and slammed my bloodied hand against the bathroom mirror over the sink.

I hated it here. I hated the building. The people.

I struck the mirror again, ignoring the burning pain from each impact.

We should never have come here. This horrible building shouldn't even have stood here. It was disgusting, and we were disgusting for being here.

I punched the mirror again, and it cracked.

Al and Mom. The nerve of them for dragging me here, for making me change everything about my life just so they could live someplace fancy for free.

I punched again. The cracks spiderwebbed out farther. I screamed, but not from pain—it was guttural. All anger and venom. All the stress welled up inside me and wanted release. It wanted to burst out of me.

Again.

Again.

The glass shattered.

CHAPTER 14

MY MOTHER SAT NEXT TO ME AND RUBBED my back. "It's only a few stitches," she said.

I stared at my hand. It was numb. The doctor had injected something into it to make it feel dead, but I could still feel the roaches crawling around inside. I couldn't stop thinking about how I had felt as I smashed that mirror. I had been so mad. Filled with rage. The thoughts I'd had. Did I really hate everyone? That moment felt so honest, but it also felt entirely detached from me. I'd never felt like that before. There was something shameful yet freeing about that. I decided not to tell Mom, though. She'd worry or decide something was wrong with me. It was better to keep my mouth shut. Ride this out, Manny.

I was good at that.

Across from me, there was a sink with a mirror. I stared at my reflection, waiting to see a roach crawling on me or out of me. It felt inevitable. I tried to distract myself by reading some of the posters in the room they'd brought us into after we checked into the ER, but nothing helped.

"I'm glad Mr. Mueller and Peter were there to help you." Mom placed her hand on the back of my head. "You should have come upstairs after you fell. You didn't need to keep working."

I had no idea what Mueller had told her, but it didn't seem like I was in trouble. When I screamed, he found me clutching my bleeding hand in a bathroom that looked like a mini crime scene. Mr. Mueller got my mother and Gracie from our apartment, took all of us downstairs, and had Peter take us straight to the hospital. Peter dropped us off at the emergency room and left without saying a word.

The real surprise was how quickly the nurses ushered us into the back to get my hand looked at even with a full emergency room. One of the nurses even offered to keep an eye on Gracie so my mother could concentrate on me. In the haze of fear and pain, it was surreal to see strangers be so kind to us.

"You should check on Gracie," I said. I couldn't look at my hand anymore. My eyes went back to my reflection. I kept trying to wrap my head around what happened. The roaches and blood. They were *inside* me. But how? I couldn't get the images out of my head. I clenched my eyes shut and tried to control my breathing.

"Manny." My mother's voice cut through my thoughts.

I perked up. "Hmm?"

"No te preocupes, mijo." She took my hand and inspected it. "I think you'll be okay, but Jesus, Manny, you can't dig into a cut if you feel something inside. You need to use tweezers, baby. You mutilated yourself. All these other scratches. You're lucky there's just the one spot that needs stitches. Even luckier they said you didn't do any permanent damage."

I didn't know what to say. I felt like I was crazy. I *had* to be going crazy—cockroaches didn't crawl around inside people's bodies. But it happened, didn't it? They were there. First the laptop and now my hand. I mean, other people saw what I saw, right? I couldn't be going crazy. But this was wrong. Roaches didn't do this; they didn't target a person this way. They lived in walls. They crawled around scavenging for old food. They didn't dig into your hand or live by the thousands in a laptop. Right? And then there was what I'd seen in the mirror. Mueller couldn't have been in the bathroom with me; the door had been closed.

"Ma . . . I don't . . ." I lowered my head. What could I tell her? "I didn't mean to do that to my hand. I just . . . I thought something was in there. It hurt."

"You panicked."

Of course I panicked—that was the only normal part of

what had happened in that bathroom. "Yeah . . . I panicked." There were roaches in my hand. The fact was sitting between us, and all I had to do was say the words, but I couldn't do it. I wasn't sure what would be scarier, her reaction or my admitting it.

"And I know the move's been hard. It's been hard on all of us. But I know this is going to be good for us too."

I wanted to take her excuse and run with it. Yeah, all of this *was* the move's fault. Her decision to agree with Al and move us almost two thousand miles away from the only place I felt comfortable was the problem. That I couldn't fit in even among other Puerto Ricans. That I couldn't visit my grandparents' graves anymore. That I couldn't get Whataburger when I felt like it. I couldn't have my socially awkward moments with Clari. It was all there, and I had every right to use those reasons as an excuse for whatever was happening to me. I wouldn't be wrong. I wouldn't be weak for it. If anything, I had a right to be angry about that. Angry enough to hurt myself. Angry enough to do anything to get back home.

Stop it, I thought. The anger wasn't good for me, and I knew that, but it felt so easy to slip into. It felt comfortable. The fear and the anger, they worked together. They made me feel better.

We sat there for a while longer. The words were right there in my mouth. The fear with its grip on my spine and the anger sitting in my gut like a rock. "I'll be fine," I lied.

"Okay, sweetie," Mom said.

"Things will be better when I get to school." Another lie.

"Exactly," she said.

I didn't know what I needed. All I knew was that the building was something I didn't need. That roach-infested hellhole in the middle of this gross town or borough or whatever the hell these people called it. I was tired of giving this a chance, but there was nothing I could do about it, was there? It felt hopeless. I was stuck in this place, and the next time something happened, I wondered if it would be worse than stitches.

Mom ran a hand through my hair. "Once things calm down, we can talk about a car, too. You got a lot of public transportation options here," she said, "but I think you should be able to handle another cheap Toyota or something."

I closed my eyes again and took a long breath. Mom was calming me down a little. "Maybe I should get a real job instead of working on the building," I offered.

"Like I said, when things quiet down, sure, if you'd like that. I know he doesn't say it, but Al appreciates your help."

"Okay. Good." Sure. Whatever. I didn't want to think about my hand, this move, or the roaches anymore.

The doctor came in and started the suturing process. "It's not a clean cut," he said. "But there doesn't appear to be nerve damage. I would avoid using this hand for a little while." He looked my hand over and then at me. "You said you had a piece of gravel in there?"

I nodded. "Yeah, um, I felt it when I put weight on my hand. I, um, panicked and decided to try to get it out."

"Understandable reaction." The doctor prepared the needle and surgical thread. "Thankfully, the worst of this is over. Those shots shouldn't have you feeling this at all, but I'm going to prescribe some Tylenol to help with the pain for the next few days. You might have a tough time sleeping tonight and tomorrow, but it will pass."

He threaded the needle and took my hand, adjusting it a little. The doctor plunged the sharp end of the needle into the skin on one side of the wound, pushed it over, and pierced the other side from beneath. "This will take time to heal. We'll prescribe you some antibiotics too, since you said you'd had a fall outside. You never know if there could be an infection." He moved the needle back and forth quickly. It didn't even register to me that he was stitching skin together. He might as well have been knitting a sweater.

I kept my eyes on the whole thing. Normally, I would have turned my head. Needles always made me squeamish, and I never watched anything gorier than a Marvel movie, but my hand wasn't all that was numb at that moment. I felt like the least I could do was watch the skin pinch together. To watch as a new scar formed. I'd done this to myself, and to turn away made me a coward, so I stared at it. I watched as the thread pulled my cut together, wondering if there was anything still inside there and what I would do if it happened again.

CHAPTER 15

I WOKE MYSELF UP THE FOLLOWING MORNING by rolling over on my hand, which sent a shock wave of pain through my arm and brought tears to my eyes.

As I walked into the hallway, I heard Al's voice. "I spoke with Mr. Mueller about the roach problem today," he said. "It's bad. You saw some of it on the eleventh floor, but the fourth floor is even worse." His voice sounded strained. "I called my bosses, and they agree with me. I . . . I think we're going to need to delay the building opening. And we're going to need to find somewhere else to stay for now."

"We need to move again?" my mother asked sharply. There was clear anger in her voice. "Al, you promised you'd make this as painless as you could. I didn't want to—"

"I know. I've tried. I can't control nature."

"I'm not asking you to control nature, Al, but I did expect you to minimize the chaos. Manny's doing worse than we both thought he would. I mean, I'm trying to keep it together, but . . ." There was a long moment of silence. "Maybe this was a mistake."

"It's not a mistake, Iris. We're living rent-free, right? We're saving for next year, like you wanted. Manny's going to have support for when he moves to college, and Gracie's going to be able to go to the school up the hill when she gets to kindergarten."

Hearing that one of the reasons for the move was so that they could save up money for my college made my cheeks flush with embarrassment. I hadn't even considered that. Part of me felt bad for being so hard on them over the big move, but then again, they hadn't asked me. If we needed more money, I could have found a job back in San Antonio. I could have found ways to save money.

"But I didn't want them to feel like we don't have a home," Mom said. "All they've known is San Antonio. They don't have friends here. *I* don't have friends here. I got a few cousins, and they haven't even called me. What am I supposed to do?"

Al let out an exasperated breath. "Oh, and I'm knee-deep in good times? They wanted renters in this place in two weeks, and look at where we are now. I'm this close to losing this job." A pause. "I know this isn't ideal, and I'm sorry—"

Mom laughed, cutting him off. "So, we're screwed one way or the other. Now we're driven out of here, and even if you get this place fumigated, you'll lose your job without renters, and then what? We're homeless."

"You know I won't let that happen."

"Do I?"

I tiptoed back to my room. Mom was right. We were screwed no matter what happened. I held my hand up—it was throbbing—and stared at the bandaging. The anesthetic they'd given me had worn off earlier than they claimed it would. None of this would have happened if we hadn't moved here. A pinprick of the anger I'd felt yesterday rose in me.

"So where do we go? A hotel? Maybe we can get some bedbugs, too," Mom said.

"I found a few rentals on the block. We'll be close."

"Those are all houses," Mom said.

"Well, some of them have the property split to accommodate two or more families," Al said. "There's one a few doors down with a large downstairs. Two bedrooms. One bathroom. We'll make it work."

"But wouldn't we have to sign a lease for that?" Mom asked. "Aren't those at least for a year?"

Al cleared his throat. "No, no. It'll just be a short-term rental. And the company is going to cover everything."

"And for how long will they cover 'everything'?"

"Fumigation shouldn't take longer than a week," Al said. "Maybe a week and a half."

"And what if it's longer than that? What if they decide not to cover 'everything' if something else goes wrong?"

Al sighed. "I don't have an answer for that."

Gracie cried out then.

"You want to get her?" Mom asked. "I'll get a bottle ready."

I waited another couple of minutes before coming out of my room. I faked a stretch and a yawn as I walked into the kitchen. "Morning," I muttered.

"How's the hand?" Al asked. "Can you still work?"

I had my back to Al, so I rolled my eyes. "Don't worry, I can handle a screwdriver if that's what matters to you." I opened the cabinet above me and grabbed a cereal bowl, careful not to use my left hand.

"Don't you two start this early," Mom said. "Eat breakfast in peace. I don't need this today."

Any sympathetic feelings I'd had for Mom or Al quickly evaporated. *She* didn't need this? Mom and Al had the nerve to uproot us completely and put us in a terrible situation, and then worry about whether I could work or if I was in a bad mood. Because, obviously, how I was doing didn't really matter, did it? What mattered was I didn't make things hard for them. They could make life hard for me, but God forbid I make a single mistake. That wasn't fair. They treated me like a prop, or worse, like a prisoner. I was locked up in this tower being told what to do and when to do it, and every time I stepped out of line, I was like a monster.

"This is such bullshit," I said.

"I'm sorry, what did you say?" Mom asked.

"It's bullshit," I said. "All of this. You're both standing there acting like I'm the problem while we're a few days away from being homeless."

"Were you eavesdropping?" Mom asked.

"It's not as if you were talking quietly."

"You're being dramatic," Al said. "Do you think I'm thrilled about the situation here? I'm trying to make things work."

"And you suck at it." I threw my arms into the air and laughed. "All this mess for nothing. They're going to fire you and then what? Then what happens, Al? You forget you have a baby?"

"Manny." My mother stepped next to me.

"No, I'm sick of this. You both act like Al's right about everything, and when he's wrong, I suffer for it? This is like when he went in on buying that stupid café with his friend. Remember that? How long did that last, six weeks? What about the car-detailing side hustle or selling all those shitty yoga pants that magically fell off a truck?"

"I was trying to keep us financially stable," Al countered.

"Oh please. Saint Alfonso. You do so much for us."

"Manny." My mother grabbed my arm firmly. "I'm not happy about this, but he is trying."

"Whatever. So, you can complain, but I can't?" I pulled my arm away from her and stepped back. "Big man Alfonso. Only thing you're good at is messing with my life and pretending you're my dad." I gripped the bowl with my good hand, squeezing it so hard I wondered if it would shatter. I didn't care, though. I was pissed off. I didn't want to be here. I didn't want to feel this way. Afraid and angry. Unsure of what was going to happen tomorrow.

Al stood up and handed Gracie to Mom. "You need to relax, Manny."

"Oh, are you mad now too?" I asked. "Because I'm right? Because you're a loser who thinks he's a winner?"

Al grabbed me by the collar and nearly lifted me off my feet. "You realize how much I sacrifice?" he screamed.

I pushed him away as hard as I could, holding the bowl aloft. "What about the rest of us? We sacrifice too."

Gracie began to cry.

My mother stormed out of the room with the baby while Al and I stood our ground. Honestly, I didn't want things to get worse, but I wasn't ready to let him get away with more of his nonsense. We'd changed so much of our lives so he could chase a few extra zeroes on a check, and all it had given us was stress and literal scars. How else was I supposed to react? I'd already taken enough on the chin, and now he expected even more from me. I was sick of letting the next problem beat me up.

"I didn't ask for any of this," I said. "And I never had a choice."

"Never had a choice?" Al rubbed his temples. "We thought this would be good for you."

"My mother thought this would be good for *you*. For you, Gracie, and her."

"No, she thought it would be good for you. I did too." He turned and lowered his head. "After your grandparents passed, you stopped being yourself. We got worried."

What the hell was he talking about? "Dude, you never once asked me how I was doing after that. Not once. All you did was pick on me and crack jokes."

"I was trying to ease the stress."

"By stressing me out?"

"It isn't my fault if you can't take a goddamn joke, Manny. You need to toughen up. You're too damn delicate. Look at you now, look at your hand. Who does that to themselves?"

"You did this," I said. "You dragged me to this disgusting place. This roach-infested hovel." I looked at the bowl in my hand—I wanted to throw it at him so bad. So I did. He ducked, and it shattered against the wall as Mom walked back in with the baby. She quickly covered Gracie's face when a few shards from the bowl almost hit them.

"Manny, what the hell is wrong with you?" Mom stared at me, wide-eyed.

"You want me to grow? To get tougher? How's that?" My hands were shaking. The pain in my left one was nonexistent.

Mom and Al looked at each other.

"Take Gracie into the bedroom," Al said.

I began to pace back and forth. My eyes stung.

"You need to calm the hell down, Manny."

Something gripped me then. All that anger finally spilled over, and I felt as if I was floating. One second I was standing feet away from Al, and then there I was, right in his face. All the fury and bile inside me boiling over. I felt like I could vomit my hate on him.

"I'm not taking this shit anymore." I saw spittle hit Al's face as I screamed the words. "Not from you or Mom or anyone. I will burn this place to the goddamn ground before I let you treat me like a piece of property again. Do you understand me? I'll burn it all. I will dance on the goddamn ashes of this place. It doesn't belong here. It doesn't deserve to be here; it deserves to be in the ground with all the other dead things."

The words didn't feel like they belonged to me. I'd never thought of anything like that before. But the anger was consuming, and it felt so good to give in to it.

"Manny," my mom called out. "How can you say something like that? What is wrong with you?"

Al stared at me and sneered. "You're a goddamn spoiled brat, Manny."

There wasn't anything left for me to tell him, and as the power from that burst of anger began to fade, I suddenly felt confused and tired. Like a switch had been flipped. None of what I'd said or done was like me. I'd never gotten violent with anyone in my life, but I'd just thrown that dish and threatened to burn down the building. I looked from corner to corner, then at my mother, her face washed with concern. I choked out a breath. I had no idea what to say.

"I need to get out of here," I said, racing for the front door.

Nobody called for me to come back.

CHAPTER 16

GRACIE WOKE ME UP AT SIX A.M. FOR THE
third day in a row.

Al had managed to get us into a new apartment in less
than two days, but the sleeping situation was rough. Grace
and I were sharing a room, and her schedule was very much
not my schedule.

I stared at the ceiling as Gracie whined. She didn't want
me; she wanted her mommy. Her mommy who could sleep
through a truck crashing straight through the living room. The
same mommy I wasn't speaking to. None of us had said a
word to each other since my outburst. I didn't hate the quiet,
but the wait to see who would talk first was hard to deal with.

Gracie's crying continued, and since I was awake, I
decided to do something about it.

"Fine," I said as I rolled out of bed. "Let's get Ma."

I scooped Gracie up and went to Mom's room. As predicted, she was in her morning coma. I gently placed Gracie down on Al's empty half of the bed, and she happily leapt onto Mom as she babbled away. Mom groggily hugged her and stroked her face, trying to lull her back to sleep. Gracie only laughed and grabbed Mom's cheeks instead.

Good. I needed a shower. Before that, I had to check if the water heater was running, because if it was, that meant Al had showered and the water was going to be cold, since this house and its property owner sucked beyond all means. I quietly headed down to the basement to avoid waking up the people we shared this house with.

Thankfully, I wasn't greeted with the hiss of the gas line or the hum of the water heater. I could take a shower for a solid fifteen minutes before the water shifted to pure Arctic temperature. Al had told Mom it was good for the skin, and I silently disagreed with him because he was the one who had us imprisoned in a shitty house down the block from the shitty apartment he couldn't take care of either.

As I was making breakfast for myself post-shower, Mom walked into the kitchen holding the baby. "Are you working at the building today?"

Whoa, more than three words. I slipped a pair of Pop-Tarts into the toaster. Because the building was closed for fumigation, Al had decided it was time for me to learn how to do yard work. I was tasked with planting bushes along the perimeter of the building and assembling a few benches and tables for the renters. Arduous work, but it kept me out of the house and away from them.

"Yeah, I've got a bunch of bushes to plant."

Mom groaned as she sat down. "Can you warm up some milk for Gracie?"

I grabbed a pan and filled it with warm water and put a bottle in it. "Al left early again?"

"Four in the morning."

Al had done a lot of heavy lifting to avoid me, and I wasn't upset about it. The few moments we were in the same room were tense. He looked at me differently. Even a bit cautiously? I couldn't fight the guilt, but it also made me angry. Everything he'd put me through coming up to New York, and he was surprised I'd snapped? Though it wasn't like I saw that moment happening either. The memory was strange. None of the details stood out, even though it had happened only days before. When I thought about it, it was like a smudged painting in my mind. Did I feel worse than I pretended for my outburst? I wasn't sure.

"What is Al even doing if he can't be in the building? Where would he go so early?"

Mom gave me a look. "He's going into the city. To the office. Trying to keep busy so his bosses don't think he's sitting on his butt while the building is tented."

I pulled my breakfast from the toaster and finished the first tart in two bites. I ignored that I burned my tongue. Too hungry and too exhausted to care. "Have you seen Mr. Mueller around?"

Mom shook her head. "I think he's avoiding me. I wanted to give his son some gas money for driving us to the hospital, but he refuses to take it."

"I can try to get him the money if you want."

"Sure, Manny, sure. Because you won't find something else to do with that money, right?"

I frowned. "You know me, always working the hustle." I put my plate in the sink. "I'm going to get dressed and head out."

Mom stared at me expectantly.

"What?"

She sighed and shook her head. "I'm too tired to get into it."

"Okay, whatever."

She wanted me to apologize, and while I wanted to, I wasn't about to be the one to go first. They owed me an apology for all of this. What I'd said was stupid and crazy—I still couldn't believe that had come out of me—but I had a right to be mad. I deserved to stand up for myself, to say what I wanted. I figured if I waited, they could see I was serious for once. If I backed down, that was typical Manny, right? I didn't want to be typical Manny anymore.

• • • •

After I finished my morning chores, I texted Sasha to hang out, who was thankfully free. I needed someone to talk to. As I waited outside Blackrock Glen for her, I tooled around on my phone. Checked my chats with Clari. I hadn't reached out to her about anything in a couple of days, not even about my hand. I didn't know how to tell her about that. Instead, I sent a "hi" with a smiley-face emoji. I looked up to see Mr. Mueller and Peter pulling up in their van.

"Manuel, how are you?" Mr. Mueller asked as he crossed the street.

"Oh, hey." I pointed at the building. "How's it going in there?" Peter was still at the van, filling a sprayer. I waved, but he ignored me. Instead, he walked to the open driver's-side window and raised the volume of his talk radio before going back to his work.

It was nice to see Mr. Mueller. He was one of the only people—he and Sasha were really the only two people—who I felt were on my side. The hand thing was bad, and while not life-threatening, it really meant a lot that he'd helped me. I didn't know what I would have done if he hadn't been there.

Mueller stared up at the building. "Why would I be in there? It is poisonous. We will go in tomorrow, when it is time to air the building out."

"Well, yeah, but don't you need to, I don't know, check it

before you take all that stuff down? To see if the gas worked?"

Mueller laughed gently. "It is best to do that once we are finished with the fumigation itself. How is your hand?"

"Better." I reached into my pocket to get the money my mom had given me. "Here. My mother is desperate to pay Peter back. You know, for gas for taking us to the hospital."

Mr. Mueller waved off the cash. "Put that away. You were in trouble. I only apologize I could not drive myself, but I cannot stand the sight of blood and was very affected by your situation."

"Well, thanks either way. I'm sorry about all the bleeding, though. I hope I didn't mess up the van."

"Only some stains, but I was happy to have to clean those up," Peter called out sarcastically.

"Sorry," I said.

Peter went back to ignoring me.

"What matters is that you are okay," Mr. Mueller said. "You went through a very traumatic event. You should not be sorry all the time."

I nodded. "It's funny, I've been feeling that way, about being sorry lately. Al and I had a big fight after all that. I keep feeling like he's waiting for me to apologize, but I don't want to. Not until he does first. I feel like he owes me that after everything I've had to swallow in moving here and dealing with everything that came from that, you know?

Even if I know I've been a little, I don't know, *off* lately."

"You are young, and sometimes that limits your perspective," Mueller said, "but I do not disagree with your assertion that you are owed respect."

"You're the only adult I know who feels that way. I feel like I'm supposed to excuse them because they're stressed out. But when I'm stressed out and hurt myself or lose my temper, I don't get the benefit of the doubt in return."

"Perhaps you are right," Mueller said. "But how often do you express what it is you want from your parents?"

"What do you mean?" I asked.

Mueller studied me. "Well, based on how you speak now, I get the impression that an apology is what you want, but what would that change? A single apology will not mean you will receive the respect you seem to want. If it is respect you want, then you need to take a firmer stance. You need to make what you desire clear. You need to admit that an apology for a single argument is not enough."

"I feel like the last time we argued, I made it pretty clear we had problems."

Mueller shrugged. "Perhaps, but it seems that you are still not being taken seriously."

"I'm not sure if I could have been more direct or aggressive. What more could I have done?"

Mueller smiled. "That is something you will need to work out, Manuel. I can only tell you so much. Only you can find a path to what you want." His tone was playful, but there was something else there.

"It's frustrating to feel this way," I said. "Like I have to keep the volume all the way up or they're going to ignore me completely."

"Then you must figure out how to make them listen," Mueller said. "If you know what you should do, then get it done. Stop trying to figure out *how* to be listened to and simply be listened to. Children's methods will only get you so far. Command respect, Manny. Do not ask or wait for it."

I felt cornered there. He had a point, but the argument had gone too far. I had crossed a huge line with Al, and I didn't want to have to cross any more to feel as if I was being listened to. It hurt to feel forced into such a big life change and like I had zero control over it. They made me feel like a child, no more in charge of my life than Gracie, and it was infuriating—more than I realized, obviously. But Mueller was right. I had to find a way. That way wasn't going to be by making things worse, but I couldn't quit. I couldn't let them be right in keeping me out of the conversation the next time they decided to make a major decision without me.

"I'll have to figure something out," I said.

A car pulled up to the curb—it was Sasha. She stepped out with a smile and shook her head. "If I had known all it took was some roaches to get that place closed up, I'd have been hiding food in the bushes all around this place."

"And good morning to you," I said.

Mueller turned to stare at Sasha. That playful light in his eyes snuffed out. "Are you a renter?" he asked coldly.

Sasha looked confused. She clearly felt something there too. "My parents are, but I'm hoping that tent never comes off."

Mueller sniffed and turned back to me. "I must return to work. If you will excuse me." He walked back to the van and said something to Peter in German.

"Nice guy," Sasha said sarcastically. "He works for your stepfather?"

"Yeah, him and his son are the exterminators."

Sasha's eyes widened. "Oh, that's a perfect career for a guy like that."

"What do you mean?"

Sasha balked. "Come on, the way he looked at me? As a Black girl, I've gotten that look from folks like him many times before. Dude's racist as hell."

I blinked. "What? No. Mr. Mueller's a sweetheart." I held my bandaged hand up. It throbbed from the movement. "His son drove me to the hospital for this." I put my hand back down; the sight of it still sent chills up and down my spine. There was a phantom feeling of the roaches crawling out of the wound, a whisper of that pain and that panic every time I looked at it.

"How very charitable of them, but you and your moms are blanquito. He'll be nice to you until it counts."

"I mean, we're not best friends and Peter's a weirdo, but they don't really strike me as that type."

"That's your privilege talking, Manny. I've seen that look a thousand times before, and I'm trigueña. God forbid I was the 'bad' type of Black person."

"Sasha, that's messed up."

"It's true. Anyway, what are you in the mood to do?"

I sighed. "Not be here?"

"That leaves us with way too many options," Sasha said.

"Yeah, I don't know, I just wanted to hang out and talk."

She snapped her fingers. "You know what? I know where we can go. We can walk, talk, and look at stupid crap. We'll even get lunch. Your treat since I'm driving."

"I'm good with that. Where are we going?"

"Yonkers, baby."

CHAPTER 17

SASHA DROVE US TWENTY MINUTES NORTH to a large strip mall with a movie theater and scattered stores. It reminded me of a smaller version of the RIM back home. It wasn't anywhere near as big, which was nice. It wasn't overwhelming and almost made me feel at home.

"What is this called again?"

"Cross County. It's a little bootleg, but they got a few things to do here."

"Is it easy to get here by bus?"

"I mean, you *can* get here by bus, but you're going to be sitting there for a long time. Aww, man." Sasha stopped in front of a boarded-up storefront with a frown.

"What?"

"There used to be a knife store here. I always liked looking at their stuff and imagining going in here one day to buy, like, the most ridiculous thing they had."

"Why?" I asked, slightly worried about the answer.

"I don't know. Fancy knives are cool. I like the way they look."

We walked around the mall for a while, content to window-shop and point out the more ridiculous products available. Sasha and I agreed that scented candles were for people ashamed of how they smelled, and we nearly got ourselves in a fight when we laughed a little too hard at a guy trying on Jordans that were way too big for someone his size. He looked like a clown. It was a relief to goof off for a while, even if it made me a little homesick.

"You looking deep in thought there, Manny. The knife thing weird you out?"

The joke snapped me out of my brain. "Oh, no. Sorry. Thinking about something Mr. Mueller told me."

Sasha took a deep breath. "I'm scared to ask."

"Nothing bad. Just . . . he said I needed to find a better way of being heard by my parents."

We walked over to a bench and sat. "What is it that you want them to hear?" Sasha asked.

"I don't really know at this point. Like, is it that I want to go back home? Would it even matter? It isn't like I have a million things back there that I care about."

"Your friends?"

I nearly laughed. "You may be surprised by this, Sasha, based on how awesome I am, but I really only had one friend."

"That doesn't surprise me at all," Sasha said, deadpan. Then she broke into a wide grin. "Jokes, Manny! Go on."

I smiled. "I mean, Clari's always been good to me. But I feel like I don't want to look clingy so soon after I left, you know?" I thought about it some more. "And it felt like we were already sort of drifting apart before I left. Maybe a clean break is for the better."

"That can happen. Just because you grow up with people don't mean you can't go your own ways for a little while, though." Sasha shrugged. "Dude, I'm protesting a building my parents actively want to live in because they think it's a good thing for *me*. I still love them. Not sure if they're loving me as much, though." She paused. "I feel you on the wanting-to-be-heard thing. There are days I feel like I could slap them with my signs or scream at them with a bullhorn, and they'd stare at me like I was a crazy person."

I laughed. "I get that."

"Wanna know what I think?"

"Go for it."

"Based on what little I know and how early we are in this friendship of ours, your beef is with your stepdad. You wear that shit on your sleeve, no matter how hard you think you're hiding it. And I get the sense that what you really want is some respect."

"That's what Mr. Mueller said, and that I need to command respect instead of asking for it."

"I don't love that we keep bringing him up or that I agree with that dude, but he has a point."

I thought about that. Al had gotten us wrapped up in his mess and had done it before. I never really wanted him to have this much control over my life. A lot of my gripes were really with him. "Ever since Al came into my life . . ." I sighed. "He wants to teach me things, like, to be independent, you know, the way a father is supposed to or whatever. To make sure I can take care of myself. Then he moves us up here, and I don't feel so independent. It makes me feel like a fricking doll or something. What kind of dad does that?"

"Yeah, but do you think you could be entirely independent? Like, if your parents had left you in Texas or left it up to you to help them decide on this move, would you have been able to make the call?"

"No, man, I'm seventeen. I'm not even built."

Sasha laughed at that. "So, Manny, what are you really mad about? What is it about Al that makes you feel this way?" She pointed at me. "I feel like once you lock that down, you'll know what you have to do to fix the situation. Or at least take a first step."

After a couple more hours wasting time, Sasha dropped me off in front of the house. I felt so much better than I had that morning, but I wasn't in the mood to go in yet.

Passing Blackrock Glen, I noticed the tenting was gone. Al stood outside on his phone and motioned me over. I almost ignored him, but curiosity got the better of me.

"What's up?" I asked.

Al ended his call and smiled weakly at me. He looked more exhausted than ever, but there was a little glimmer in his eyes for a change. "We're all set to move back in," he said.

Oh wow. I'd thought we'd be in the temporary space for at least a week. "Like, today?"

"More like tomorrow night. We're going to need help moving some things back, okay?"

I nodded. "Yeah, let me know what you need." I wasn't sure how to feel. On the one hand, the temporary housing situation sucked, so it'd be nice to have my own room and hot water back. But my mind flashed to the various fucked-up moments I'd had living at Blackrock Glen. When I looked at the building, all I could see were cockroaches. While the fumigation gave me some comfort, was it guaranteed they wouldn't come back? I hated the other place we were at too, but at least I hadn't seen a roach there. Blackrock Glen could be clean as a whistle, but what good would that do for the memories and bad dreams? If I thought about it too much, I could feel the sensation of the roaches inside my hand, the sting of my skin separating as they crawled out of me.

Al stared at me a moment and then cleared his throat. "Are we good?"

I thought about that. Were we good? I wasn't a hundred percent sure. Then again, Al had succeeded for once. He'd worked hard and kept his word to Mom. The bags under his eyes were the signs of that, weren't they? And this was an apology. Maybe not the exact words, but I could see he wanted us to get past the outburst, and I was feeling the same way. The bowl. The screaming. None of that felt like me, even if I was still mad about this move. I thought about Mueller and Sasha. The advice they gave me made sense, even if I had a lot to work out on my own. Being there, with Al opening a door for me, though, I had a moment of realization. I had to take a step forward too. Just like Al had.

"Yeah," I said. "I'm, um . . ." I took a long breath. "I'm sorry about before."

"Me too, kid. Let's move past it."

"Got it. Thanks."

"Oh, I was looking at the shrubs and outdoor furniture. Everything looks fantastic. Excellent job." Al gave me a quick thumbs-up. "I need to call the building inspector back. We'll talk later."

"Uh, sure, yeah."

Was that a compliment? I decided it was best to walk away then. No telling how long a compliment from Al would last, so I might as well make the best of it and ride that wave for as long as I could.

"Yo, Manny."

I cringed. I knew that voice. There went that good-vibe wave. It lasted, what, thirty seconds?

Frankie called out again as he crossed the street. "Manny." He was stone-faced. Thankfully, he was alone.

I stopped walking and turned. "Yeah?"

"That's all you have to say?"

I had no idea what he was talking about. "I'm sorry, what?"

Frankie narrowed his eyes. "Like I didn't just see you coming out of Sasha's car before?"

Why would he care that I was spending time with Sasha? "What?" I asked again.

Frankie leered at me. "'What?'" he said mockingly. "The hell were you doing in her car?"

Why was he so mad? Was he jealous? "Are you guys a thing?" The only time I'd seen Sasha and Frankie interact, it felt very much like she couldn't stand the sight of him.

Frankie clenched his jaw. "You didn't answer the question."

"Dude, we were spending time together. As friends." I narrowed my eyes back at him. "Like, I'm sorry, but I didn't think you two were a thing. Sasha didn't say anything."

"Watch your mouth." Frankie puffed up his chest and stepped closer.

I took a step back. "Hey, I'm not trying to make you

mad; I'm saying we were hanging out. Nothing serious."

Frankie pulled his pants up and spit. "Typical blanquito behavior, man. You really think you're better than everyone you meet, don't you? You think you don't need to even try to have respect for the people you meet."

What was I supposed to do, curtsy when I met people? I'd had enough of this nonsense. Screw this guy. Here I was, trying to have an enjoyable time with a friend and take in the rare compliment from Al, and along comes this tool to ruin my day. As I thought about it, I realized I'd gotten a compliment from Al because I'd stood up to him. I'd shown Al that I could stand up for myself, and he had clearly respected me for it. Now this guy was stepping up to me for completely assumed—and wrong—reasons, and I was supposed to back down from this? I was supposed to be scared and walk away? The anger I'd felt when I'd exploded at Al filled me. This time I welcomed it.

I stepped toward Frankie; I wasn't going to back off this time. "Dude, from day one, you and your friends have been ragging on me and acting like I owe you respect. Why? What makes you think I owe you anything? Since I'm new here, I'm supposed to bow down to you?"

I could tell Frankie was giving that some thought. He eyed me up and down. Probably wondering if I was playing a trick to get him to come at me.

"Come on. You're the badass, right? You're the one who

wants respect? Take it, then." I knew that was crazy. I knew that was ill-advised, but I couldn't help it. I felt drunk on this feeling.

"Talking a lot of shit," Frankie said. He stepped forward with his hands up, as if ready to throw a punch.

I flinched. For all my talk, I flinched. The confidence I'd felt disappeared, and just like that morning at Blackrock Glen, I was left feeling disoriented. I stumbled back, my heartbeat pounding in my ears.

Frankie spread his arms out, laughing. "All bark and no bite. Punk-ass." He squared up again. This time wasn't going to be a bluff.

A horn sounded off to my right. I turned my head. It was Mr. Mueller's van.

Mr. Mueller rolled down the passenger-side window and leaned over. "Manuel," he said. "Would you be able to assist me with something at the building?"

I straightened up and stared at Mr. Mueller, not knowing what to say. "What?"

"Your stepfather asked for me to move a few supplies, and I could use your assistance, young man." Mueller gave me a stern look. His eyes moved to Frankie, the look hardening even more. "Please, get into the van. We can drive the rest of the way."

"You lucky," Frankie mumbled as he backed away. "Lucky as hell."

I didn't feel lucky, but sure. I'd fallen into Frankie's trap, and he made me look—and feel—like a complete loser. The high of getting Al's apology and compliment was replaced by the defeat of having an old man save me from an ass-whupping.

I walked over to Mueller's van.

CHAPTER 18

"YOU ARE FIGHTING?" MR. MUELLER SAID.
"Seems to be a worthless endeavor."

"That wasn't really a fight," I said.

"The other boy did not seem to share your sentiment,"
Mueller said. "Around here, many your age behave like
that." He sniffed with disdain. "Are you trying to fit in? Letting yourself be corrupted?"

"What? No." I shook my head. "No. These guys are
just . . . They've singled me out because I'm not *completely*
like them. I stood up for myself."

Mueller nodded. "What did you stand up for?"

"They make fun of me. And now Frankie was accusing
me of trying to get with Sasha. I don't even like her like that."

"Mistreatment." He licked his lips and pulled the van

over to park in front of the building. "I understand it must be hard to have peers treat you like a pariah, but I do not believe acting like them is the proper response. Can you not see that you are better than them? I am sure there is more that you can do to remove their presence from your daily routine."

I stared ahead. "What? Should I call the cops? Tattle to my parents?"

"Those with authority would accomplish more than lowering yourself to a savage act," Mueller said. "What good is it to act like an animal? What does it benefit? Do you feel good about fighting?"

"No," I muttered.

"I cannot hear you."

"No," I said a little louder. "No, it doesn't feel good, Mr. Mueller. But it . . . I don't know what else I can do with all this." I grabbed my chest. "I've got nowhere to put all this anger and stress. So, maybe it feels a little good when I do it, but after, no, I feel like garbage."

Mueller eyed me with a smile. "One as young as you, perhaps your perspective is that life is very hard, no?"

I snorted. "Yeah, something like that."

"I came to this place impoverished. I could not speak the language. Americans, they took every opportunity to remind me of that. They used the wars fought in Germany to label me something to hate." He scratched at his hands. "It made me angry, but I learned to use that anger. To allow the fire to burn as I saw fit."

"Did it help?"

"It did. At first. Unfortunately, there will be those who simply cannot live up to what your expectations are. I decided to stop caring about that and care about myself and my family. I made a loving home for them, and I worked extremely hard to maintain that, despite whatever savages I faced down. That boy, the one you wanted to fight. He does not deserve for you to stoop to his level. You are better than that."

"Funny enough, he said my problem was I thought I was better than him and his friends."

"Perhaps you are. Look at what your family is bringing here." Mueller motioned to the building. "A new home for the people of this neighborhood. A blessing. Something stable and clean. Something unburdened by years of neglect. If there are those who would not be grateful for it, that is not your problem."

"People here wouldn't agree with that. They say we're gentrifying the neighborhood. That building isn't for them."

Mueller looked confused. "What is that? 'Gentrifying'?"

I sighed. "They say we're only going to rent to people with money and force everyone out of here. It happened in Manhattan forever ago and then in Brooklyn and Long Island City, I think. They bring in luxury buildings, and the neighborhood sort of shifts."

Mueller's eyes widened. "I do not understand. Why would the people here leave?"

"They get priced out. New businesses are too expensive to buy from. The rents go up. Other developers come to buy up lots." I shrugged. "I sort of get it, but I also don't? Like, why be mad that the neighborhood would get better?"

"Hmm. Indeed. A place like this could benefit from new money." Mueller scratched his chin. "I too have trouble understanding why the neighborhood would not benefit. This building is more of a good thing than I even predicted."

"Maybe," I said.

"No, no. Things will be good if what you say about new money is true."

"I have doubts," I said. "If what Sasha and everyone else says is true, they'd force you out too. Would you be able to move your home and business?"

Mueller stared into the distance, thinking. "I would not want to be forced out, but I do not believe I'd be in danger. I have survived for a long, long time here. This is my home. It will always be my home, despite however many invaders may try to move me. I will always be a survivor."

"Am I an invader?"

"Ha. No, you and your family are welcome." Mueller sighed. "When I was young, I fought as well. I was angry, but I also believed in my fight. I believed in my struggle. I understand you want to stand up for yourself, but there are other ways to do that than immediately resorting to violence." Mueller held up a finger. "Is that boy an obstacle for you? Truly something to fight against? Does he represent an injustice?"

I shook my head. "I mean, if you're talking about an injustice, the only one I can think of is being moved to a new state against my will. Frankie, I don't know, he comes with it. If I hadn't been forced to come here, I never would have had to meet him or deal with his crap."

"Is that truly an injustice? The move has been good for you. It keeps your family with food and security. You may not like what your stepfather does, but he does not do it with ill intent. And as for your issues with him, there is no honor in hurting the rest of your family to earn his respect or get revenge on him for the slights you feel you have suffered against him."

He wasn't entirely wrong, and I felt a little bad getting riled up about the move again so soon after coming to peace with Al, but I couldn't let it go. At the end of the day, I felt like I had no choice about where I was, and those thoughts kept digging themselves deeper and deeper into me.

"I guess I should head home and start packing my stuff up—Al said we could probably move back into our apartment tomorrow." As I was getting out of the van, I had a thought: the only times I ever felt okay about Blackrock

Glen were when I was around Mr. Mueller. "Hey, do you and Peter need any help?"

"Perhaps," he said. "Peter and I only need to clean and check for more nests. It is not exactly fun work, and I am sure your stepfather has other priorities for you."

"I can fit both into my schedule," I said. I wasn't going to admit it, but I wanted to be around someone I felt comfortable with.

"Very well. We can use the assistance."

"Will the three of us be enough to inspect the whole building like that?" I asked. "Al mentioned an inspector."

"An inspector?" Mueller seemed surprised. "I suppose that makes sense. For our part, I will see about bringing in some young men like you. It will be fine."

"Okay, great." I closed the van door. "See you soon. And thanks, uh, for the advice and the help with Frankie."

CHAPTER 19

I SAT UP ON MY BED. MY HEART WAS pounding. I couldn't breathe.

Gracie. Oh my god. Gracie.

I jumped from my bed and raced to her room, plowing into her crib. The jostle nearly woke her, but she was fine. Thank God, she was fine. It was another nightmare. In the dream, I saw her being taken away by roaches. She was cooing so happily, fist in her mouth, as they swarmed over her and carried her off, taking her away from me. All I could do was watch, some unseen force keeping me from walking. I clenched my eyes closed and tried to find my breath again. I sat on the floor and stared at the ceiling. What the hell was I going to do with myself?

Above me, movement. I saw three little brown roaches

crawling toward the light fixture. They crept into an open joint in the ceiling and disappeared.

Later that day, I was walking out of Blackrock Glen when Sasha ran up to me. "Manny, hey," she said as she stopped and caught her breath. "Sorry, I don't do the running thing. You move back in?"

"Not entirely, though we slept in the apartment last night. I'm just glad the building's going to open."

"Well, one step closer to finally being neighbors." She gave me a closer look. "Hey, you doing okay?"

I laughed. "Ironically? Slept terribly."

Sasha eyed me with suspicion. She seemed to read me. "Is that all?"

I shuffled my feet. "After you dropped me off, Frankie came up to me and tried to start something. He wasn't happy we were together."

Sasha crossed her arms. "Because he thinks we're dating or something?"

"Well, are you dating him?"

She laughed. "Oh please, we hooked up at a dance last year, like, it wasn't that serious."

"He seemed pretty fricking serious about it with me. Like, I was pretty convinced you two were a thing and I didn't know."

Sasha's eyes widened a little. "Yeah, but it isn't that

serious. I don't even text with him. Like I said, we kissed, but whatever, it was a dance, and everyone was having fun. I thought he saw it the same way. The way he acts when he sees me, if it were like that, he would say something, I think."

"So really, you're saying you ghosted him after a hookup, and he's completely in the dark about how you feel versus how he probably feels."

"Pretty much."

"Yeah, well, it wasn't fun getting wrapped up in whatever drama there is."

"And you're mad at me for that?"

"A little?" I stuffed my hands into my pockets. "And I know that's stupid. Totally do, but it still annoyed me."

"Shouldn't Frankie be the one you're annoyed at?"

"Oh, I'm pissed at him, too. Don't worry about that."

"And now you're pissed at me?"

"No, not at all. Look, I'm sorry. He came at me when I really didn't need to get my legs kicked out from under me."

"Well, I'm sorry. For real." Then Sasha smiled wide. She was excited. "I got good news, by the way." She leaned in and squealed. "My petition worked—Blackrock Glen has to set aside a certain number of units for folks who need housing assistance. It isn't a massive change, but it keeps the building management company from making the place its own little walled garden." She gave me a gentle slap on the shoulder. "See? Petitions work, man. People listened."

"Uh, that's great." I was too exhausted to process what she was saying, though I could tell my response was not what she was looking for. Peter pulled up to the curb ahead of me, and I was glad to see him. "Can we talk later?" I asked her.

Sasha nodded and watched as I jogged over to the van. I knocked on the passenger-side window, then waved.

Peter looked at me and slowly rolled down the window. "What do you want?"

"Sorry, just, uh, I was looking for your father."

"Why?" he asked.

"I needed something to do."

Peter scowled at me. "You realize we're professionals, right? We're not your babysitters or your friends." He shook his head. "You act like you can waltz on over whenever you want and waste our time. We're working, kid."

"Mr. Mueller said I could help. I wanted to lend a hand."

"Then maybe get your ass back to your apartment and let us finish what we need to do," Peter said. "We're on cleanup. We got a few floors left. We got some extra hands. We don't need your help." Peter's expression shifted, and he looked past me. "Ach, hallo."

I turned to see Mr. Mueller standing behind me with a tight smile. "Manuel. How are you?"

Mueller felt like he was on top of me, as if he had been there the entire time. I stepped back and bumped into Peter's van.

"Watch it, man." Peter stepped out of the van and walked around the front. He looked past me to Mr. Mueller. "This one says you told him he could help."

"That is correct, Peter," Mr. Mueller said. He turned to me. "Thankfully, it is extremely easy to clean unoccupied apartments. We simply need to ensure surfaces are mopped or wiped down. The windows must remain open a little longer, but I would say it was quite a success."

"Is it common for roaches to survive the fumigation?" I felt awkward asking. "I think I saw one crawling around in my apartment. Or maybe more than one. More like a few, really."

Mueller narrowed his eyes and shook his head. "I will check, but I would not worry. Perhaps one or two are still dying, but the infestation should be cleared up."

"Did the inspector approve of everything? I overheard Al say they came last night, but that was all."

Mueller smirked. "*I* stand by my work, Manuel."

"Right. Sorry."

"No apologies, boy. You are right to ask." Mueller waved to the building. "The others are working on the ninth floor. You can help them. I believe you should all be able to get things done quickly. Take a floor at a time, clean up as per my instructions, and your stepfather will finally have his building back."

"You sure you don't need me to help you?"

"No, Manuel. Head up to the ninth floor—the others will show you what needs to be done."

I entered the building through the front door and called the elevator. As the doors opened, I scanned the space to make sure it was empty—it was. Mueller said people were working on nine, but I decided to go to the tenth floor. I remembered that was where I'd left off when I was fixing kitchen cabinets, so I figured I could do Al work and Mueller work at the same time. The elevator doors opened with a happy little ring, and I stepped out. I heard music. Salsa. I followed the music to an open door.

"Hello?" I called out.

The music was coming from one of the rooms inside. I followed the sound to what I knew was a bathroom. The door was closed. I knocked—no answer—and went to push it open. There was resistance, as if someone were holding it closed, but when it did swing open, nobody was behind it. Instead, someone was standing in front of the tub with their back to me. They were shaking from head to toe, but the room wasn't cold.

I lingered by the door. "Hey, are you okay?"

The person slowly turned. It was Frankie. He looked like he was having a seizure.

"Holy shit!" I stepped into the room, but no closer. "Frankie? What's wrong?" I turned to look over my shoulder and yelled, "Help! Is anybody else up here?"

Frankie's eyes were closed behind his goggles. Had he inhaled something? He couldn't have—he was wearing a mask over his face. I noticed it then, on his neck and his hands, wherever he had bare skin: roaches. They were crawling up to his head and creeping under his mask. I flashed back to the night in the basement when I'd felt the roaches crawling all over me, right before I'd met Mueller.

Frankie's eyes suddenly snapped open. He closed the gap between us and grabbed my arm hard. His fingers dug into my bicep with enough force to make my arm go numb. The shock made me feel like I wanted to jump out of my own mouth.

"Dude, what the hell is wrong with you?" I pushed him away, but Frankie kept his grip.

"Frankie, let me go!"

Frankie didn't answer. I pushed at his face, trying to get him off me. His mask slipped from its position, exposing his nose and mouth. They were covered in roaches. Some of the bugs ran into Frankie's mouth, others into his nostrils. Nausea washed over me. My hand throbbed where my stitches were, my body going into fight-or-flight mode from the memories flooding over me. I had squeezed a ton of roaches from the cut in my hand, but not nearly as many as were crawling into Frankie's body.

I tried to pull away again, but Frankie was too strong. I swatted at errant roaches that crawled onto me, terrified they would try to go into my own mouth. I kicked at his legs and crotch, desperate to get away as the insects continued to crawl into his mouth, nose, and ears.

I kicked him hard enough in the knee to force him to fall back. His grip finally loosened, and I took the opportunity to pull away. I scrambled out of the apartment into the hallway, slamming the apartment door shut behind me. I held on to the handle and pulled back with all my body weight to keep Frankie from getting out while using my other hand to get my phone. I dialed my mom first, but nobody picked up. Then Al. No answer.

What if something had happened to them, too? What was I going to do?

I felt a pull on the door, and it opened a crack. Frankie was trying to get out.

I pulled as hard as I could, but I could feel my grip on the door handle slipping. If I lost this tug-of-war, I realized I had to be ready to run. I dialed Sasha.

"Hey, Manny. What's up?"

I went to speak, but my sweaty hand lost hold of the doorknob. I fell back against the opposite wall—hard—and dropped my phone. The apartment door swung open, and Frankie lunged at me, grabbing me by the shirt collar and pulling me to my feet.

"Manny?" Sasha's voice was faint.

"Get help!" I screamed. I kicked Frankie's knee again, and he lost his footing enough to let go. This time I wasn't going to wait. I sprinted to the stairs and threw the door open, nearly falling head over heels down the first flight. As I reached the ninth floor, I lunged at the door, but it opened before I could get my hand on the handle. It was Peter, followed by his father. I collided with Peter, which might as well have been the wall.

"The hell is wrong with you?" Peter pushed me away.

I gasped for air. "Thank God. Upstairs, Frankie. He needs help."

Mueller looked concerned. "What happened? What were you doing on the tenth floor?"

"Please. Just please. Help him."

I turned and led Peter and Mueller upstairs. I was terrified, but we had to do something.

When we got to the tenth floor, the hallway was empty. From the apartment I'd run out of, I could hear that someone had turned up the music. Looking at Mueller and an incredibly annoyed Peter, I motioned to the apartment and slowly walked over.

I peeked inside; Frankie was mopping the floor. He stopped cleaning and looked our way.

"Oh, hey guys." He waved. "Mr. Mueller, how are you?" Frankie held out my phone to me. "You dropped this, dude. I found it in the hall."

I looked around the room. No roaches. No sign of a struggle. "I don't understand."

Peter groaned and pushed me from behind. "Cute joke," he said, and left.

"I swear to God," I said, turning to Mr. Mueller. "He needed help."

Mueller smiled softly. "No worries, Manuel." He gently patted my arm. "But isn't it nice to see the both of you getting along? It is so much better when you don't fight, no?"

CHAPTER 20

LATER, I STARED AT MY REFLECTION IN THE bathroom mirror. I opened my mouth, trying to see down my throat. I looked up my nostrils, terrified I'd see a roach's antennae moving in them. I ran my fingers over freckles and moles on my face and arms, trying to remember if they'd always been there.

Just then, I heard the front door fly open. "Manny!" my mom cried. "Are you here?"

I came out of the bathroom and met her and Gracie in the kitchen. "Uh, yeah? What's up?"

"Oh my god, baby, are you okay?"

"I'm okay."

She looked me up and down, searching for signs of injury and finding none. "Then why'd you text me '911'? And call me so many times?"

After leaving Frankie, Peter, and Mr. Mueller, the only thing I could think to do was track down my mom. "I just . . . I saw a bunch of roaches, and I freaked out."

"Manny! You almost gave me a heart attack." She clutched her chest. "If you see a roach, you call Al or tell Mr. Mueller. You don't text me '911'—that's for emergencies only."

"I'm sorry. But I mean, if the fumigation didn't work, shouldn't we do it again?"

I knew I couldn't tell Mom everything, but she could convince Al to talk to Mueller and close the building one more time. There was something wrong with this place, and as crazy as it may have sounded, it was coming after me. How soon before it set its sights on Mom or Gracie? She wouldn't believe me about Frankie, but I was telling the truth about the roaches.

"I'll have Al talk to him, but based on what I've seen, Manny, I think you're overreacting. I haven't seen a single roach since we moved back in, gracias a Dios." She emptied the clothes dryer and headed to her room.

I didn't know what else to do. I had seen those things spill out of me and crawl into someone else. They were real, and they were still in the building.

I was desperate to tell my mom the truth. But what was I supposed to say? The cockroaches in the Bronx liked to live in human hosts? Mom clearly wasn't going to take me seriously. Or if she did, she'd send me to a therapist.

And then she'd look at me differently, not as her kid but as a failure. A problem child all screwed up because she made a few mistakes when she was younger, marrying my dad and having me. It would be easy for her to look at her good marriage and her new kid and let me fade away, wouldn't it?

And whenever I thought about telling someone with the power to lock me away about all the weird moments and the nightmares I'd experienced, well, I was certain they were going to lock me away. Nobody in their right mind would believe me.

Hell, I'd lock myself up.

I knew I was stressed out. I knew I was done. I didn't understand why these things kept happening to me. Normal people got panic attacks or headaches, didn't they? They didn't see roaches everywhere. They didn't squeeze them out of their hand.

I realized I hadn't gotten back to Sasha. The last she'd heard from me, I'd been screaming for her to get help. I texted her.

I need help. Please.

My phone chirped.

Manny, Jesus Christ! What happened?!

Hard to explain. Can we meet up?

Come downstairs. I'm on my way there.

U r?

Yes, asshole! What do u do when a friend calls u in a panic? Just go back to playing video games?

I couldn't help but smile.

Be down in 5.

My mom came back into the kitchen. "Anyway, it smells amazing on some of the other floors," she said. "What are you using to clean?"

"Huh? Oh, I'm not sure what they're using," I said. "But maybe Al can ask Mueller when he asks about the roaches."

"Well, I'll mention it to him, but he's waiting on that inspector's report. That guy's dragging his feet."

"What does the inspector do, exactly?"

"They inspect the building."

"For what?"

Mom shrugged. "Ay, sweetheart, I have no idea. I guess to see if the place is safe to live in." She nodded at my phone. "Talking to Clari?"

"Oh, uh, no. I was texting Sasha. I'm about to go meet her."

Mom made a face.

"She's a good person, Ma. Besides, it's not like I'm trying to date her or whatever. She's going to be a neighbor, and I don't hate the idea of having a friend in the building."

"Oh yeah, real good neighbor. With her petition."

"But it worked, didn't it?"

Mom frowned. "So now we get people on assisted living here like it's the projects?"

"Isn't that good, though? Let some of the locals have a chance at living someplace comfortable and safer?"

"And who made the neighborhood uncomfortable and dangerous?"

Oh wow. I was not ready for that. "That's, uh, that's pretty ignorant, Ma."

"That's the way things are, Manny."

"Then that's messed up."

"The world is messed up. We all find a way to survive. That's the only way."

I shook my head. "I don't want to believe that."

"Why?"

"Because then it gets way too easy to give up hope."

I expected her to laugh at me because, honestly, I would have laughed at me. But she just gave me a sad smile and headed to the sink to do some dishes. It was ridiculous that I'd even mention something I felt completely devoid of. Hope. I didn't have any, but that didn't mean I wanted to yank it away from everyone else.

Al walked into the apartment, typing on his phone. He crossed to Mom and gave her a kiss on the cheek. He looked my way. "Everything good?" he asked.

I was tempted to tell him about the roaches, but I didn't want to make Sasha wait. "I'm good. You?"

"I'm not." Al leaned against the wall opposite me. "This inspector hasn't sent me or my company a damn word back on the status of the building. He promised I'd have something last night."

Mom sighed.

I stood and put on my slippers. "And?"

"And I'm freaking out that he's going to give me yet another reason I can't open this place."

"And I was just saying to him that his little friend didn't help matters either," Mom said.

Al shook his head. "No, but that's incredibly low on my list. Fine. She won. I don't have time to drive myself crazy about that."

It was a relief to hear Al wasn't going to go after Sasha. What she'd done was a good thing.

"Well, I'll see you later," I said.

"See you later, kid," Al replied.

I walked past him.

"And Manny?"

"Yeah?"

"I know it's been crazy, but I really do appreciate all you've been doing." He scratched under his left eye. "Even if you're a pain in my ass."

That was shockingly big of Al. "Oh, um, yeah. You're welcome."

"You gotta be kidding me." He slipped a shoe off and slammed it on the counter. There on the sole, the green-and-brown remnants of a roach. Al gritted his teeth. "That old man told me the job was done."

"You were right, Manny." Mom shook her head.

"You saw more of these?" Al asked.

"I just told Mom about it. She was going to talk to you."

"Where did you see them?"

"Gracie's room. On the tenth floor too."

Al closed his eyes and rubbed them with his hands. "I'm going to run into traffic. Oh my god, I'm going to run into traffic and hope a truck gets me. All that fumigating. Getting the bosses to pay for the lodging down the street. The time wasted. That man's going to get me fired."

That wasn't fair to Mueller. "Mr. Mueller said there might be some stragglers," I said. "I think it's more about the building than—"

"No, Manny. That man and his weirdo kid lied to me. They told me the job was done. They told me they found nothing. It's not even twenty-four hours later, and here we are."

"Look, maybe if you talk to him again."

"Talk to him?" Al laughed. "I'm *done* with him. He's fired. With this inspector, the damn low-cost units, and now this? No, no, no. I'm not taking three losses in a row. He gets not one damn dime of my money unless he fixes this. And if he doesn't, then I'll sue him into the goddamn sewers with all these roaches."

My phone chirped.

Here.

"I'm sorry, I gotta go," I said. I couldn't be in this building anymore. If I wasn't feeling terrified for my life, I was filled with so much anger that I wanted to punch a hole in every wall. This place was eating at me, and a few hours away would feel like a luxury vacation.

"Go, go." Al shooed me off.

I grabbed my things and gave Gracie a quick set of kisses on each chubby cheek before heading out.

CHAPTER 21

I SAT ON THE BLEACHER STEPS AND STARED out into the dark of the trees ahead. There were loud pops in the distance. "Those are guns?" I asked.

"Yeah, they got a police firing range somewhere over there behind the parks." Sasha laughed. "And this is the rich neighborhood. These people feel safe knowing those dudes are blasting off right next to them."

"That's terrifying."

"Dude, what's going on? You freaked me out before."

I took a breath. "You're going to think I'm crazy."

"Dude, I'm a seventeen-year-old with nothing better to do than wage a one-woman war against a building management company I can't even name."

"I appreciate that, but . . . this is hard for me to say."

"Well, you're going to have to, so say it."

I searched for the right words. "Since we moved here, weird, scary things have been happening. First, I found roaches in my laptop, like, literally they were *in* my computer. And way more roaches than should fit in a laptop. Then in the basement, there was this huge infestation of them, and I don't know, it felt like they were coming after me. When I cut my hand? I saw roaches coming out of it. And earlier, when I called you, I found Frankie with them all over his face." I paused, picturing what had happened and wishing I hadn't. "Sasha, they were crawling into his mouth and nose and ears. I know this all sounds crazy. But I know what I saw. I *know* it."

I waited for Sasha to laugh at me or simply grab her stuff and go. But when I looked at her, I could see that she was trying to process what I'd said.

"Was there anybody with you when any of these things happened?" she asked.

"Well, with my hand, Mr. Mueller. And then there was Frankie." I pulled my shirt off one arm to show her the bruises.

Sasha stiffened. "What did he do to you?"

"He grabbed me, and the roaches were everywhere." I shuddered. "But then two minutes later, he was fine. He acted like nothing had happened. And I know something happened because I watched a few hundred roaches crawl into his mouth." I put my shirt back on. Talking about what I'd seen gave me gooseflesh.

"Have you talked to your parents?"

I scoffed. "They'd lock me away."

Sasha nodded.

Awkward silence came crashing into the scene.

I stared at my feet. "I think the building's dangerous, Sasha. I'm worried about what happens when people finally move in. What if someone gets hurt?"

Sasha sat up straight. "Look, I believe you believe you saw these things, but you're telling me that the roaches in the building are what? Demonic? Like, they have an agenda?"

"I don't know, I just . . ." I grabbed my head. "You need to believe me, Sasha. Something is really, really wrong. I mean, Mr. Mueller just fumigated Blackrock Glen, and the building is still filled with roaches."

"Are you saying the roaches can't be killed?"

I shook my head. "No, they can totally be killed. I've killed a ton myself." I thought about what Al had said about Mr. Mueller and Peter, that they had lied to him about the job they'd done. "I think, well, if the roaches are still alive, then Mueller and Peter lied, didn't they? They didn't do their job. Why? Why wouldn't they do their job?"

Sasha leaned forward. "You think they have something to do with all of this?"

"Maybe? But then, I'm fairly sure there was an exterminator before Mueller. So, what, did he suck at his job too? Is the Bronx just full of scamming exterminators? Or are the roaches at Blackrock Glen, I don't know, immune to whatever chemicals they're using?" I paused. "I'm having a tough time believing Mr. Mueller is a crook. He seemed really excited for Blackrock Glen to open. Plus, he genuinely cares about the Bronx—why would someone who lives in the neighborhood—"

"What do you mean 'lives in the neighborhood'?"

"Mueller and Peter, they live, like, five doors down and across the street from the building."

"Mueller might live in the Bronx, but that old man does not live in that house," Sasha said.

"What are you talking about? Al said he was right there."

"I don't know where your stepfather got that idea, but Mueller is not from Blackrock Avenue. I can tell you that with certainty. No way in hell."

"Are you sure?"

"Manny, I've been sitting in front of that building since last year, and I have only ever seen Peter walking around there. The mean old man? I didn't see him until you and your family showed up."

"That makes things a lot weirder, doesn't it?"

"A lot frigging weirder," Sasha said.

Things fell quiet between us. I realized there was one more thing I needed to tell her.

"I want to apologize to you," I said.

She gave me a confused look.

"For earlier, when I came at you about Frankie—that wasn't right." I opened and closed my right hand while staring at my bandaged left hand, trying to release some of the tension I was holding on to. "Like, right now, sitting here with you, I feel calm and normal. But when I'm around Blackrock Glen, I feel like I want to fight all the time. I have all this anger, which is totally not me. And I'm not trying to make excuses—no matter what I'm going through, I shouldn't take it out on you. Honestly, I shouldn't take it out on anybody, but it was wrong of me to get mad at you."

"Well, Frankie's a dick. He's good at getting people riled up." She smiled at me. "But I appreciate the apology."

At that moment, I was so grateful to have Sasha as a new friend. "So, what do we do now?"

"Honestly, I'd stay away from Mr. Mueller if I were you. From the moment I met him, something was off about that man. Worse than his son. At least that guy actively hates everyone he sees. Mueller seems like he's hiding something."

"Yeah . . ." I was stuck. Why would he lie? Mr. Mueller was a good guy . . . wasn't he? Other than Sasha and Heriberto, he was the only person in the neighborhood to show me any kindness.

Why would he want us to think he was from the block when he wasn't?

CHAPTER 22

I NEARLY CRAWLED OUT OF MY BEDROOM in the morning. Talking with Sasha had helped, but it hadn't wiped out the memory of what I'd seen with Frankie. That was fresh in my mind, fresh enough to keep popping up every time I closed my eyes. With my eyes open, every shadow, every little movement, made me think the roaches were there, crawling, twitching, and skittering. I'd barely slept.

Coming out of my room, I found Mom reading a book in the living room while Gracie played. Mom looked exhausted too. "Good morning," she said. "You think you can help me with finishing up the benches outside today?"

"Hey," I said to Mom as I gave Gracie a little smooch on the top of her head. I ran my fingers through her hair and checked her toys to see if there were any signs of roaches near her. She was the most helpless one. The perfect target. "I can help with that. Where's Al?"

"Downstairs firing Mueller," Mom said. "Al said he found even more roaches in the basement last night. He went apoplectic."

"That sounds bad."

"It was very bad."

"Should I go downstairs now?" I asked.

"Why?"

"I don't know." Something didn't feel right. I needed to go down there. If just to make sure everything was okay. "I'm going downstairs. I'll start on the benches."

"Don't get involved with Al's business, Manny. I know you like that old man, but he is not your friend."

A part of me believed that, but Mr. Mueller had been kind to me. Was it really my problem if he'd lied to Al? What was I even thinking? Of course it was my problem. The roaches in this building had attacked me more than once. I was annoyed at myself for thinking that way. Al was right to fire Mueller if Mueller had lied. We needed to fumigate this place.

"Don't worry," I said. "I'll mind my own business."

My phone chirped. A text notification from Sasha.

Hey, be there in five. I found something.

Outside, I made a beeline for the benches to finish the work that Mom mentioned, thankful I could see Al across the street in conversation with Mueller and Peter. I couldn't help it—I was curious. Things did not look very friendly. Al was moving his hands the way he did whenever he gave me a lecture. Mueller was stone-faced. Peter reacted once or twice, but Mueller turned to settle him down. I decided it was for the best to do my work, but as soon as I picked up the first piece of prefabricated wood, I felt that weird *Somebody's watching me* feeling, and sure enough, I looked to find Mueller glaring at me.

Awesome. Al had to have mentioned I was the one who saw the remaining roaches.

"Hey," Sasha said as she walked over. "Need help?"

I stared at the ground and nodded. "Uh, yeah. Hold on to the seat here so I can Allen wrench these pieces together."

"Looks like your stepdad is flipping his shit across the street."

"I'm trying not to pay attention."

"Manny," Al called out.

"Crap," I muttered.

"Manny, come here."

"You want some backup?" Sasha asked.

"Yes, please." I put the bench materials down and gathered myself. It wasn't a big deal. I had told the truth, and Al was doing the right thing. Mueller hadn't done the job he'd been hired to do, and we needed a real exterminator to take care of business.

Sasha and I walked across the street. When I was close enough, Al motioned to me and then to Mueller.

"Manny, what did you see?"

"Uh, where?" I asked.

Al gave me a *Come on* look. "In our apartment, Manny."

"Oh, uh, I saw roaches in Gracie's room and in the kitchen."

Al pointed at me. "You see? Then I go downstairs last night, and what do I find?" Al held up his phone. There was a video of a clutch of roaches in the basement. It had to be dozens. Al shook his head. "Then I decide to look at some of the stuff you two left behind, and color me surprised when I see the chemical you're using hasn't been legal since the goddamn eighties."

Sasha's eyes widened. So did mine.

"The both of you must see why I'm having a problem with this," Al said. "You're jerking me around. For all I know, whatever you sprayed in that building was useless, or worse, incredibly harmful to the people I'm going to have living there."

Mueller grimaced. "You are blowing this out of proportion."

I looked at Peter. His energy had shifted. He was no longer mad. If anything, he looked relieved. He leaned against his van, already accepting everything Al had said.

"So, I'm crazy?" Al asked.

"No, you are simply ignorant of how this works," Mueller said. "Sometimes these processes take longer than anticipated."

"You told me the roach problem would be solved."

"I told you we would do our best."

"I paid for a solution," Al barked. "Not for a goddamn con artist to come in and take me for my cash while getting me fired."

Mueller frowned. "If you are unsatisfied—"

"Unsatisfied?" Al laughed. "I'm pissed off. What *you* are is fired. You don't see a dime from me, and I want your crap out of my basement immediately." Al turned in place and laid eyes on Sasha. "Oh god, please tell me you're not here to gloat."

Sasha blinked. "That wasn't my intention, but I mean, if you want me to. I was hoping to find out how many apartments were going to be affordable."

Al rubbed the space between his eyes and bit his lip in thought. "Two floors, okay?" he said with exasperation. "Manny, you and your friend can go now. Thanks for confirming what you saw."

Mueller looked confused. "What does she mean by 'affordable' apartments?" he asked.

"Blackrock Glen is setting aside units for people who normally can't pay rents as high as they are in this condo," Al said. "For that to happen, though, means a little more scrutiny from the city, and since you didn't do your damn job, I'm the one who gets to deal with the fallout."

"That's right, Mr. Mueller. 'Affordable' means people from this neighborhood have a chance to stay in this neighborhood," Sasha added.

I gently pulled at Sasha's arm. "Awesome. Great. Maybe we go now."

Mueller crossed his arms and rubbed his chin. "I have seen this before. 'Affordable' units. For the unsavory elements."

"I'm sorry, what did you say?" Sasha pushed me away.

Mueller made a face. Sasha's reaction clearly amused him.

"Sasha. Come on," I said.

Sasha shook her head. "No, I'd like to get this man's thoughts on this."

I saw Peter shake his head slowly.

"The people who can afford to live in that building intend to help this community. To enrich it. They will bring life here. Unfortunately, there are others I already see who will not do the same." He stared at Sasha. There was a deep, simmering anger in his eyes.

"You know a lot of those affordable units go to people your age," Sasha said. "Retired folks who can't afford ballooning rents. They have a fixed income. They need help."

Al nodded at that. "She's not wrong."

Mueller snorted. "Ah yes, retirees. But their children and grandchildren. They will cause problems."

Now I had to say something. This was getting uncomfortable. "And you believe that because?"

Mueller shrugged. "I suppose I have made up my mind based on my experiences."

"So have you made up your mind about me?" I asked.

"You are a good one," Mueller said. "Your potential is vast. I would not compare you to the others." He looked back to Sasha. "Especially not to troublemaking trash."

Al stepped in. "Whoa, whoa. Easy there. These are kids. You shouldn't speak to them that way." He looked at me again. "Go upstairs, Manny. I need to finish up here."

Sasha stared at Mueller, her eyes wet and red.

This time I pulled at Sasha's arm a little harder. "Sasha . . . let's go."

She finally relented, and we crossed the street.

Back in the building, Sasha paced in the hallway. "I told you that old ass was racist as hell."

"You were right. I'm sorry. That was . . ." I threw my hands up. "That was exactly what you said it was."

"And that stuff about the chemical he was using." Sasha stopped and pointed at me. "I looked them up on Yelp— Peter and Mueller—and I found next to nothing. There were, like, two Yelp reviews, and I'm sure Peter wrote one of them."

"Seriously?"

"Yes, seriously, and, Manny, what if those chemicals are as harmful as your stepfather said? What if that's why you had those episodes?"

That wasn't really a crazy idea. "Yeah, but I had those experiences before Mueller used them on the building," I said.

"I guess that's true," Sasha said. "For all we know, he planted the roaches in the building and was aiming for the job before you all even got here." She crouched down and rubbed her eyes. "We need to find proof, though."

An idea popped into my head, and I opened my mouth before I could give it any more thought. "We can check Peter's property. Maybe there's something in the yard or in the garbage. Let's go now while they're still arguing with Al." I stopped myself. "That's insane, though. We can't do that. That's, like, totally illegal, right?"

Sasha stood back up. The smile on her face was worrying. I looked back outside. Al and Mueller were still fighting; Peter and the van were gone—that was a bonus. We'd only need to get past Al and the old man.

Sasha and I quickly walked toward the house and doubled back once we were out of sight.

"They're going to see us," I said.

"Not if we sneak in through the neighbor's yard. You can hop a fence, right?"

"I mean, is that something you're an expert at?"

"Dude, it's a fence. Everyone's hopped a fence at least once."

I followed Sasha as we crept toward Mr. Mueller's neighbor's driveway. Nobody was home—I hoped—and we quickly passed the house into the backyard. The fence into Mueller's yard was about waist height. Sasha easily hopped it and checked the line of sight between where Mueller and Al remained arguing and where we were standing.

"Come on," Sasha said. "They won't be able to see us from where they are if we stay out of the driveway."

I inelegantly climbed over the fence. Mueller's backyard was a mess. There were weeds and overgrown grass and junk scattered all over the place. I nearly tripped over a rusty tricycle as I walked over to Sasha. The back of the house had wide windows with no curtains, leaving the inside clearly visible. It looked barren. No wall decorations, little furniture, and thankfully, no people. I got closer and put my face to the glass. I was looking into someone's bedroom. It was sad. Just a mattress, some disheveled sheets, and a little lamp. The carpet was dingy with a huge brown stain at the foot of the mattress. It didn't seem like Peter or Mueller really cared about upkeep, or furniture for that matter. I glanced to my right and saw six garbage cans, all filled to the brim, next to the back entrance.

I quietly walked over, and Sasha joined me. One of the cans had a torn bag; it was filled with boxes of what looked like an electronic product. I pulled the bag open a little more and took a box out. "The hell are these?"

Sasha shrugged. "I'm not sure." She dug into another can. "There's mousetraps in this one."

I opened the box and pulled out a little white gadget that had its own plug. It had rounded edges on the front end and slits at the top and bottom. I looked at the back of the packaging, and there was a description saying this thing would "make pests go away with an ultrasonic sound!"

I looked back in the bag I'd found the gadget in. There had to be dozens of those things in there. "All of these boxes are sealed. Why would they be in the trash?" I checked the other cans. No normal garbage—it was all rodent and insect repellents: sprays, traps, gels, and other weird chemicals. Nothing was open. Maybe this was the way Mueller stored his equipment?

"Dude, none of this stuff looks like it's been used, like, ever." Sasha looked disappointed. "I think if we want to find out anything important, we have to go inside."

Suddenly I heard car doors closing and Peter and Mr. Mueller talking—shit. Sasha and I locked eyes as I pocketed the little sound gadget. We crept along the back of the house and hid around the corner. I held a finger to my mouth to make sure Sasha stayed quiet. She rolled her eyes, like, *No, duh.*

"Warum bist du losgegangen?" Mueller asked the question loudly. He was audible from where we were.

"There was no point staying," Peter said. "The *Sopranos* reject found us out."

"So, you are giving up?" Mueller's tone of voice was so different. It was harsh and laced with anger.

"My mother raised me to be smart and know when to back away," Peter said. "I told you if you wanted to do this, you should let me do it. I could have given us a lot more time than what we got." Peeking around the corner, I saw him come into view and head for the back entrance.

"No. I will not discuss it further."

"We're going to get caught, Opa."

My heart was pounding. We were pushing it. I slowly edged along the side of the house toward the front yard and motioned to Sasha to follow. She grabbed my arm, holding me in place.

"What if we can find out what they're up to?" she whispered.

"Too risky," I answered.

"Manny . . ." Sasha raised her eyebrows.

"If you abandon me, yes. You told me you would help me. You promised." Mueller sounded closer.

Peter walked deeper into the yard, and Sasha and I pressed our bodies against the side of the house. He had his back to us—thank God. "I didn't . . . You told me we'd do this before anyone got involved. Now there are people involved."

"Do not worry about them. Help me. Help me do this."

"Aw, crap," Peter said as he walked out of sight toward

the driveway. "Something got into the bags out here. Let me clean up and we can talk inside, okay? I think I can get you what you want."

"No . . . no . . . ," Mueller said. "Things have changed. It is a shame to hear that they planned to let undesirables in that building. That means the plan must change."

"What does that mean?"

"It means I need to think more, and we will talk when you are done."

"Um, okay." I heard Peter riffle through the bags we'd been looking through. "Did Al say when we needed to get our equipment out of there?"

"By tomorrow morning."

"And he'll probably lock us out of the building then. Does that ruin your changed plan?" Peter asked.

"Nein, nein. We will merely set the dominoes. I assure you we will not need to worry. We will succeed."

"Okay, Opa. Whatever you say."

I heard keys and the back door opening, along with Peter rummaging in the garbage cans. I looked at Sasha, who nodded, indicating it was time to get out of there— that was enough snooping. I turned to see if we'd been eavesdropping while Mueller's neighbor was watching us, but the coast was clear. Sasha and I hopped back over the neighbor's fence, then quickly made our way off their property and speed-walked away from the houses. Once we were farther down the block, I stopped and realized my heart was beating as if we'd sprinted for an hour.

I turned to Sasha. "What the hell was that?"

"Is it bad that I expected the house to be more of a murder house?"

"It could have been if we hadn't gotten out of there."

"Yeah, but now we know more about them, don't we?" Sasha noted.

I nodded. "The hell do you think he meant by 'the plan must change'?"

Sasha took a deep breath. "Let's go back to my apartment. We can talk this over and research some more. I don't know what's going on, Manny, but whatever it is, I'm beginning to think you're right about that building not being safe for anyone."

CHAPTER 23

I STARED AT THE POSTERS ON SASHA'S walls. They weren't for bands or movies; they were for politicians. All local people serving in the Bronx and other New York City boroughs.

"I knew you were political," I said, "but this is something else."

"Hey, we all have our thing." Sasha sat at her desk and typed on her laptop. "Come look. This is what I wanted to show you when I came over earlier."

"What is it?"

Sasha passed her laptop to me. On the screen was an arrest report for Peter Crull.

"Is that our Peter?" I asked.

"Yep. Address is 243 Blackrock Avenue, and his description matches too. Our boy's last name ain't Mueller, and he has a penchant for lurking. Got arrested multiple times for trespassing and criminal mischief. There's something in the reports about flammable materials. I'm guessing he was creeping in the company car or something."

I blinked. "The hell is 'criminal mischief'?"

"What they charge white boys with when they want to give them a slap on the wrist."

I pulled a chair over and sat down. "Okay, but why would Peter have a different last name from Mr. Mueller? Do you think they're not operating on the level? Maybe Peter's arrest record makes it hard for him to get jobs, and he had to come work for his dad."

"That's my guess too. The old man hired his loser son because he had no other prospects. Maybe there was a divorce, and Peter took his mom's name or whatever. That happens all the time. Now Peter's dad's back in his life after Peter did a bunch of stupid stuff, and Mr. Mueller's propping him up or whatever."

"You really think that's all this is?"

"Maybe?" Sasha shook her head. "But if you're working like this, wouldn't you take lower-profile jobs? Like, it's insane to take a job in a big building. There are more people to notice the stuff you and I are noticing."

I nodded and handed Sasha back the laptop. "Let's say this is all true," I said. "This guy helps his weird, criminal son make a living because he can't hold a real job. But Mr. Mueller legit knows how to be an exterminator—I mean, he's not a total con. Why not do the job?"

"I have no idea," Sasha said.

"What if we dig more into Mueller? He said his first name was Gerhard. That can't be a super-common name these days. We can find out more about him."

Sasha started typing again. "You mind Venmo-ing me thirty bucks?"

"Why?"

"Because I need to pay an ancestry site to find the connection between Peter and Mueller. Then we can start narrowing things down."

I pulled my phone out and sent the money. "Done. We already know how they're related, though. What good does this do us?"

Sasha scrolled on her laptop. "Well, if we're investigating whether these guys are, like, frauds, that's the first thing I'd verify, right? He could just be saying Peter's his son."

"I guess so." I rubbed my eyes. "Sasha, what if we're digging for no reason?"

Sasha narrowed her eyes, clearly annoyed with my suggestion. "No, nope. Manny, Al said Mueller was using a banned chemical. If there's even a small chance that he and that dweeb son of his are part of why people could get hurt, then we need to investigate this."

"I totally agree with that, but just us?"

Sasha nodded. "Yeah, man. We build a case and bring it to the right people. Do you really think that if we go to someone now, they'll believe us?"

Point taken. "That makes sense. I'm sorry."

"Don't be sorry. Work. Stop getting in your head and being trigger-shy about doing the right thing." Sasha went back to her laptop. "Hold up. This doesn't make sense." She looked confused. She typed some more. "I don't understand this."

"What's that?"

"It says here that Peter's father is Peter Crull Senior. Which means Pete's a junior."

"Then who the hell is Mr. Mueller?"

"Peter's grandfather."

That was odd. Why would Mueller tell people that Peter was his son? "Maybe Mueller raised Peter? But there's no way that guy is old enough to be Peter's grandpa."

Sasha kept typing. "Pete senior has been dead for a long time, but it looks like Peter's mom is very much alive. Born Ariane Mueller-Crull in 1952. Which makes her in her seventies."

I worked the rough math in my head. "Wait. That can't be right—Mr. Mueller is at most seventy."

"Well, Ariane's father looks to be Gerhard Mueller, born in 1915." Sasha looked over at me. "That racist look like he was born in 1915?"

I shook my head. "Is there a way to look up immigration records? Maybe there was a clerical error." If Mueller was born in 1915, he'd be over a hundred years old. The man was old, but he was certainly not a century old.

"Already ahead of you. Found a site where I can request records. Let's see what we get back." Sasha typed. "I'm trying to see what else I find under Gerhard Mueller as well. There are dozens of them, but none match up with what we're looking for." She sighed. "This sucks, man."

"At least you're finding things out. I wouldn't even know where to start with any of this. I'm still processing fifty percent of what I've seen so far, and now this? How is everything about this building and these men so weird? What the hell is going on?" I rubbed my hands together and stared at the ground. "This is what I get for not doing my rosary. My grandmother always said I should do the rosary every day, and I laughed her off, and, like, look what's happening now."

Sasha narrowed her eyes. "Okay, Manny, first, calm down. Second, I don't understand what any of what you said means."

"The rosary," I said. "You know, you do a bunch of Hail Marys and then an Our Father." I thought on that. "Maybe the creed, too?"

"I'm nondenominational."

"So, you don't pray at church?"

"Not like robots."

"Fine. Whatever. I'm not about to talk about Catholic mass when I don't need to."

"Wise words," Sasha said. "Wait. What? No . . ." She continued typing.

"What?"

"Wait, wait, wait. Holy crap, I don't know if this has anything to do with our situation, but this is crazy." She turned the laptop around to show me a news story. The headline read, BRONX FIRE KILLS 12, INCLUDING ARSONIST.

"Okay, so what's that?" I asked.

"It's from 1981," Sasha said. "Says there was a fire set in a building in the Bronx. They found the body of the arsonist among the remains of the building. Turns out he was a suspect in nine—*nine*—other fires." She looked at me. "Dude, this is wild. The name matches: Gerhard Mueller."

"Wow. That's an insane coincidence."

Sasha kept scrolling. "It gets crazier," she said. "Jesus, Manny, the last fire he started was on Blackrock Avenue. Right where Blackrock Glen now stands."

"What?" I couldn't help but scoff. That was more than insane—that was impossible. "Now you're playing with me."

"Nope. According to this, Mueller was a local exterminator working in the neighborhood for a building owner who was later found guilty of hiring people to burn his properties down for the insurance money. They would hang balloons filled with a flammable liquid and then light a little fire. It made the source untraceable. Mueller, though, ended up lighting himself on fire this time. He went right up with the building."

I stood up. "Jesus."

"This stuff happened all the time back then. The neighborhoods were wrecked, filled with people who were left behind by the rest of the city. Nobody gave a shit. Too many Black and brown folks. Not enough white faces to care."

Sasha went back on her typing spree. "Got the obit for Gerhard Mueller. It's a short one. Says he was survived by his daughter, Ariane, and grandson, Peter. That's it. There weren't any other Muellers in the ancestry profile either. Well, aside from his wife, but she died in 1971."

"Are there any pictures? That might help."

Sasha shook her head. "Maybe a newspaper archive?"

"How do we do that?"

"We keep digging," Sasha said as she typed. "Other papers had to have reported the fires. Let me check the *Post* and the *Daily News*. The first one we got was the *Times*. The other ones might have posted pictures of the asshole who started the fires." Sasha typed more. "Damn it. The other papers reported the story, but none of them has a picture of Mueller."

"Sash, I want to make sure we're both thinking the same thing."

Sasha closed her laptop. "I'm thinking . . ."

I could tell by her pause that she was thinking what I was. "That our Mr. Mueller is the same guy who died in the fire in 1981. Meaning, a century-old arsonist has come back from the dead . . . to resume life as an exterminator?" The words had sounded preposterous in my head and even more so out loud.

"When you say it like that, it does seem kind of ridiculous. But I don't know, dude. There are so many coincidences. And if the things you said happened to you really did—"

"They did," I said.

"—then is it so hard to believe that we're dealing with some paranormal shit?"

There had to be a way to figure out who Mueller really was and what he wanted. "What if we cornered Peter?"

"I'm not sure," Sasha said. "You yourself said he's got a mean streak. If anything, he might be all in on whatever Grandpa is up to." She tapped her fingers on the edge of her desk. "What about—" She stopped.

I waited. "About . . . ?"

"What about Peter's mother? What if we found her and spoke to her?"

"We tell her that her father is maybe back from the dead and is living with her son?"

"No, no, no. We fish for info. She will have pictures of

him. First things first: we gotta figure out if our insane theory is even true."

"And if it is?"

"Maybe there's something about Mueller's history that will reveal what he's up to or at least help us understand how this all even happened. Maybe knowing what led to Mueller's resurrection, or whatever you want to call it, will tell us what our next step should be."

I didn't have an argument against the point that Sasha made. All I wanted was to understand what was going on, and as Sasha noted, having information was better than flying ignorant. Besides, the more concrete info we had, the more likely that people would believe us if we had to tell them what was going on.

"What about our parents? I mean, Al and my mom aren't the most open-minded people. Maybe your dad or mom?"

Sasha sighed. "Dude, my mom would lose her mind if I mentioned anything demonic or demonic adjacent in our house. And my pops is too skeptical of anything and everything to care. Unless Mueller showed up at our house in a bedsheet floating ten feet off the ground, nothing would convince him this was anything more than the two of us being super jumpy about an old white dude."

She was right. There was nobody we could really rely on to believe us. We needed evidence that would confirm our claims, or at the very least, make it clear that there was a threat to Blackrock Glen.

"Where do we start?" I asked.

"Well, we find out where the daughter lives."

"You really think that would work?" I was doubtful, but I couldn't think of a better idea.

"I'm open to anything else you come up with, but this lady's the only person who can give us the real story."

"If she talks."

"If she talks." Sasha sighed again.

In my periphery, I saw movement. Tucked in the corner of her room was a cockroach. I gingerly crossed to Sasha's desk and picked up the little gadget we'd found back at Mueller's house.

She looked up at me from her chair. "What are you doing?"

I looked to the corner, and she followed my eyes. The roach was still there.

"Aw, hell no," Sasha said.

There was a rolled-up manual in one side of the gadget under a plastic flap. I opened it and read through the instructions. I was to plug it in and then press and hold the largest button at the front of the device for five seconds to "initiate its auditory functions."

Sasha pointed to an outlet, never taking her eyes off the roach.

I plugged in the device, held the button on the front of it, and looked over my shoulder to watch the roach. After five seconds, a little green light stuttered to life.

It was immediate. Pain in the center of my chest and in my neck. Like a knife pulled through my lungs up my throat. My tongue flattened, and I gasped for breath. I retched, but nothing came up. The pressure in my chest was immense, so much that it felt like my ribs were going to burst. I fell onto my hands and knees, my arms scratching at my neck. I rolled onto my back, and it made things worse, a weight bearing down on me that was suffocating. I fought to get back on my knees and retched again. This time, something in my throat shifted, and a wad of phlegm flew out of my mouth.

I sensed Sasha by my side and could tell that she was screaming, though I couldn't hear her. I retched again and more phlegm came out of my mouth. I wasn't vomiting; I was hacking something up. Before long, the pain had moved from my chest to my throat, and more came—thick, brown gobs of phlegm. Thank God, the pain started to subside. Before long, there was nothing left to hack out. My throat was raw. I tasted wet dirt in my mouth. Hints of grass. Like I'd chewed up a lawn.

Once I could see straight again, I sat up and saw how soaked my shirt was. I dripped with sweat. It fell from my hair to the carpet in a steady stream. I took long, hungry breaths, ignoring the pain, and focused on what I'd coughed up. The phlegm was moving.

"Jesus, Manny." Sasha was crouching next to me. "Are you okay?"

I pointed weakly at the device.

Sasha yanked it from the wall and knelt beside me. "What the hell was that?"

I couldn't answer her. Instead, I could only stare at what I'd coughed up. The pile of phlegm bubbled. It twitched. A writhing mass of brown and shiny shells, wet carapaces, and black legs. Roaches. The same kind of roaches from the building. The same I'd seen in my room. The ones that came swarming from my hand.

The roaches had been inside me all this time.

"Now do you believe me?" I said weakly.

"I believe you, Manny," Sasha said. "This is some cursed shit." And with that, she crushed the roaches under the heel of her shoe.

CHAPTER 24

WE SAT OUTSIDE SASHA'S APARTMENT. AFTER we'd cleaned up my mess, she'd suggested we get some fresh air. It was beautiful out—not too hot, a nice breeze—and I realized that I felt better than I had in a long time. My throat was raw as hell, and my abs felt sore, but my mind felt clear. Still, I couldn't help but dwell on what had just happened. Those things had been inside me this whole time. Living in me, growing in me. My god, were they eating me from the inside out? Laying eggs? Who knew how long those things had been in me?

Sasha looked over at me. "Do you need a doctor?"

"I don't think I need someone poking around my body right now." I nearly laughed, but my throat hurt. It felt like someone had dragged razors down my tongue and all the way to my stomach.

Sasha didn't laugh. "Do you think Mueller is the one who did this to you?"

Did I? Had Mueller ordered an army of roaches to crawl inside me? "Honestly?" I felt like I was trying to find a breath that wasn't there. "I don't know. Everything you found is pointing to something crazier than I could ever imagine, and I threw up roaches. At this point, anything's possible."

"Well, we'd know more if we could speak with his daughter. There's, like, no trace of her on the internet. It's like *she's* a ghost."

I nodded. And then I realized something. "Oh shit, Frankie! Frankie's got those things inside him, too!"

"We gotta help him, Manny. He's an ass, but he doesn't deserve to have roaches all up inside him."

"We'll find him and corner him or something and plug in one of those devices." I tried to remember what we'd heard earlier when we were hiding in Mueller's yard. "What did Mueller say?"

"The racist stuff or the evil stuff?"

"No, the stuff about his plans. If he did do this to me and Frankie, then could this be part of his plan? Like, maybe this is his way of brainwashing people or making them do things they normally wouldn't."

"You said you didn't feel like yourself whenever you were at Blackrock Glen," Sasha said. "Outside of the physical stuff, are you feeling better?"

I thought about that. "I can't really tell." I rubbed my temples. "We can figure that out later, but in the meantime, if Mueller is doing this to other people, maybe there's a way we can help them *and* expose him."

"Expose him how?"

"Sasha, you're my witness. We can tell everyone on the block what's going on. My parents. Even the police."

Sasha mulled that over. "I don't know. It'd just be your word and mine. After the Melvin mess, I don't think many people on the block are going to buy into anything I have to say again."

"Who the hell is Melvin?" I asked.

"The guy before Al. He was the one who got the building put up over the parking lot that was there before," Sasha said. "Friend of a friend of my dad's—which is how my parents found out about the building. He came off like a creep the one time I met him, but I figured when he dropped off the face of the earth, maybe that was a good thing. But the building wasn't going anywhere, and then they hired your stepfather, so I decided to start protesting."

"But hold up, the building that Mueller died in was there before, wasn't it?"

"Yeah. Like I said, it was a parking lot."

"So, if that was where Mueller died, maybe the construction on the new condo woke him up. Like, they disturbed his grave and there he was, all angry at a new building being built over the remains of the one he wanted burned down."

"And his creepy grandkid still lived on the block."

"Yep, so he had someone to go to."

"And the roaches?"

"I haven't gotten that far yet. I'm not sure I'm ready to."

Sasha nodded. "We still need more. We need to understand this man and whether there's anything we can do to stop him. Right now, all we have are guesses."

"Then we need to find Mueller's daughter," I said. "I have an idea."

Sasha leaned against the steering wheel of her car and laughed. "I can't believe you were right about the phonebook thing. Like, *everybody* used to be listed in those. Isn't that crazy?" She laughed again. "And people whine about privacy now. Back in the day, I could open that book and find out about you in five minutes."

I'd suggested we try to find Ariane with a phone book from the library. It took all of fifteen minutes to find her. As it turned out, Ariane lived about an hour from us in a town called Croton Falls. I may have sucked with computers, but I'd learned enough about archaic nonsense from my grandparents to know a thing or two about paper-based stuff.

"To be fair, we found out about this entire family on the internet in an hour," I said.

"Yeah, but the effort of looking people up in a book. An actual paper book, dude. The more I think about it, the more surreal it sounds." I could tell Sasha was desperate to ease the tension. She kept looking at me with this expectation. Like the roaches would burst out of me at any moment.

I didn't blame her. I felt the exact same way. I needed to stop thinking about Mueller, even if we were minutes away from his daughter's place, getting ready to ask her about him. It was too much to handle. Too much not to pretend for a few minutes that we were still seventeen-year-old kids trying to have a normal summer—whatever normal would be after all of this.

So, I kept it going. I wasn't going to kill the flow. "To be fair, phone books were useful. It wasn't like you could remember forty numbers off the top of your head."

"My moms could. She still dials everyone she knows on her old-lady landline phone without even looking. It's like a superpower. Blows my mind every time."

I thought on that. "You know, I was going to make fun of that comment, but I can barely remember what I had for breakfast, so remembering entire phone numbers sounds like trying to memorize calculus equations with my eyes closed."

"The internet ruined everything," Sasha said.

I scoffed. "That's a lie. Tell me how long you'd last in 1989. Looking up people in a phone book. Having to use the newspaper to find out when a movie was playing."

Sasha yelped. "What?"

"Yeah, my mom told me. She said when she was a kid, they had to use the newspaper to look at the times. Then they called to see if the show was sold out."

"Barbarians."

"I have no idea how people survived back then," I said. "Like, imagine having to sit and talk for the entire time you're with someone."

"We're doing that right now."

"Yeah, but, like, if we were sitting down in a house, we'd need to talk."

"I mean, they had books and TV," Sasha noted.

"And commercials."

"Disgusting."

"Prehistoric times."

The conversation petered out then. I synced my phone to Sasha's Bluetooth and put on some music. She was not a fan of DeBarge.

"How old are you again?" Sasha asked.

"This is good."

"Every time I think I understand you, Manny, you do something that really makes me wonder whether you're, like, a crazy person or a time traveler or a cop pretending to be a teenager."

"Blame my mom."

"I already did."

"How close are we to this place?" I looked out the window. We were in a nice little neighborhood. The houses were big but close together. It was strange—I always assumed the houses were close in places like the Bronx because of the lack of room, but it appeared people liked being on top of one another all over New York.

Sasha looked at her GPS. "Says two minutes. And you got the story, right? We're ready to do this?"

"We're students at Bronx Science, and our summer assignment for journalism is to research a local historical event. Since we live on Blackrock Avenue, we picked the fire from 1981."

Sasha sank a little into her seat. After I rattled off our story, it didn't seem like we had any hope of getting past the threshold of Ariane's home.

"Should we turn around?" I asked.

Sasha remained quiet and then sighed. "We have to do this. This woman might be able to give us something we can use. Whether it's proof or, like, I don't know, a story about her dad that could get to him?"

"You think it'll be that easy?"

"Absolutely not. But I brought my knife just in case."

"Jesus, Sasha, don't bring that with you."

"What if she's a racist arsonist too?"

"What are you going to do with a knife in a fire? Stab it out?"

Sasha chuckled. "Always so stupid."

"It's stupid for me to believe you could stab a fire?"

"No, I'd protect us." Sasha smirked.

"By stabbing a woman in her seventies?"

"I'm not planning to."

I started to laugh. "We're going to get the cops called on us."

"You're saying don't bring the knife?" Sasha pointed ahead. "I think that's the house there."

Ugh, we kept getting interrupted by real life. "Now I'm nervous."

"Same, but we're here. Worst case, she tells us to go away."

"Unless you pull the knife."

"That's, like, plan K."

We got out of the car at the same time and walked over to the house. It was a two-floor monstrosity with actual columns at the front door. I rang the doorbell and stepped down off the stoop. I didn't want to chance being too close and freaking anyone out before I even made a first impression.

"Oh, crap." Sasha ran back to the car and returned with a book bag. "We're here for homework, right?"

"Good call," I said.

The door opened, and a friendly-looking older woman stood there with a soft smile. "Hello? Can I help you?"

I smiled back. "Hi, so sorry to bother you. Are you Ariane Mueller-Crull?"

The woman nodded.

"Um, hi. My name is Manuel"—I motioned to Sasha—"and this is Sasha. We're hoping you might be able to help us. We're researching a fire that took place in our neighborhood, and—"

"This is about my father." Ariane's smile faded, but she didn't look mad.

"Yes, um, we're sorry. We had an assignment and found out you lived here, and while I wouldn't want to intrude or dig up old pains, we were hoping to get a direct account of what happened."

Ariane gently nodded. "And they're making you do this for school? In the middle of summer?"

"Journalism class," Sasha said. "Part of learning how to get information from direct sources. And it's a supercompetitive school."

Ariane took a long hard look at both of us, then turned, motioning over her shoulder. "Come in, then. I can talk for a little while."

Sasha and I looked at each other. She mouthed, *For real?* I shrugged my response. And then the two of us walked into the house of the daughter of the would-be ghost haunting my luxury condo building.

"You want anything to drink?" Ariane asked. "I've got some soda in the fridge that I never drink." She turned to us with a joyless grin. "Just in case my son decides to finally visit."

Well, there was something. Ariane and Peter weren't the best of friends. That made me wonder if she even knew Peter was traipsing around with his very dead grandfather. I had to assume she didn't. If she knew her father was around, she wouldn't invite two strangers in to talk about the things he'd done while he was alive. Or at least I hoped that was the case. This family might not have been very rational, and I had to keep that in mind.

"I'll take water, if that's okay," Sasha said.

"Nothing for me, thanks."

Ariane got Sasha a glass of water and sat down in front of us. She pulled an ashtray over and lit a cigarette. "I try to keep these to three a day. After a meal. Sometimes I make exceptions, though." Her fingers—stained orange on the tips—made it seem like there were a lot of exceptions. "Okay, you want to know about the fire. About my father ruining this family?"

"Ms. Mueller-Crull, if it's a problem, we're happy to leave you alone," I said. I didn't mean it, but I didn't want to push her either.

"No, no, no. It's fine. More people should know about what happened. My father killed people. He even managed to kill himself in that last one." She laughed coldly. "My father used to talk about his dignity and his hard work." It didn't feel like she was lying about that. She seemed almost eager to speak to us. Maybe she'd never had the chance to air all this before. I couldn't imagine what it was like to have a family history like hers. It had to take a toll. I felt a little bad then. She didn't deserve this. I guess Peter didn't either, even if it seemed like he was itching to help his grandfather carry out whatever it was he aimed to do.

"Why do you think he set those fires?" Sasha asked as she opened her laptop. "Did he really need the money?"

"That's a big question," Ariane said, and shrugged. "I don't really know. The money shouldn't have been a problem. Dad's business did well. Well enough that my late husband was able to keep things going until he died. Then Peter and I took things over once Peter turned eighteen. It's not what I'd wanted—for myself or Peter—but with Pete gone, it just made financial sense." She grimaced. "A few years after that, he decided he was the big man who had to run it himself."

"So, if Gerhard didn't do it for money, then why?" I asked.

Ariane took a long drag off her cigarette. "Right before I had Peter, Dad was robbed. It was Christmas, and he'd finished a big job. His pockets were bursting, and I suppose people noticed. That was when it started."

Sasha shifted in her seat. "What started?"

"The anger. He began to blame everything on the African Americans or the Puerto Ricans or the Dominicans—whoever was easiest. All working-class people, but to him, they were the same as the men who robbed him. I always told him he couldn't be sure the guys who robbed him were Black, white, or green, but he didn't care. He was so sure that these people were his enemy. That they didn't deserve the same chances he got." Ariane ashed her cigarette. "And it's not like he was alone, and it's not like I haven't had my moments." She looked at Sasha. "Though I'm not that kind of person, you understand."

Sasha raised her eyebrows and forced a smile. "Oh yeah, I understand."

I cleared my throat. "Um, well, so he was angry and decided he'd burn down buildings as revenge? Doesn't that feel extreme?" I couldn't begin to understand why any of that would seem logical. People had attacked me before, and I'd wanted to get back at those people, but I'd never thought about wanting to hurt someone's whole family or, like, an entire community.

Ariane leaned back in her chair and sighed. "He thought he would scare people out. That he got money was a bonus. Who knows? Maybe he quite literally saw it as payback. Maybe he was always that way. That hate doesn't just pop up, you know? It changed everything I ever thought about him, honestly. Completely shifted my memories. Was my father that kind of monster?"

"What was your answer?" I asked.

Ariane stared to the side and frowned. "I realized that he was. He was always that way. He wanted an excuse to let it out, and those poor people were right there."

Sasha looked at me and back to Ariane. "I'm sorry if we're dredging bad things up."

Ariane shook her head. "No, no, no. It's fine." She stared at her hands. "Peter and I moved here after everything happened. Nobody wanted to see our faces on the block anymore. Peter moving back always bothered me. After Dad died, I'd kept the house and rented it out. When Peter turned eighteen, he asked to move into it. He worshipped that damn man, even if he was a toddler when everything happened."

"I was close to my grandfather too," I said. I wondered if *my* grandfather came back from the grave, what I would do to spend time with him again. What would I do to make sure he stayed? To make sure he accomplished his goals?

"Is your grandfather still alive?" Ariane asked.

I shook my head. "No, I lost him a little over a year ago."

"Was he a good man?"

"I hope so," I answered.

Sasha sat up. "So, um, what you said about your son idolizing him . . ."

Ariane's eyes widened. "Would he follow in his grandfather's footsteps? I hope not, but sometimes I'm not so sure." Her eyes got wet. "He has the same temper as my father. The same way about him. It's so strange too. Peter was four years old when it happened. I kept it all away from him, but after a while I had to tell him."

"That had to be hard," Sasha said.

"It was. Peter never really reacted to it." She shook her head. "I remember once he asked me to come with him to lay flowers where the old building burned." Ariane sniffed. "I couldn't do that. It didn't feel right." She wiped her eyes with the backs of her hands. "Give me one second." She left the room.

Sasha turned to me. "I feel like we're next to something, right?"

"Yeah," I said. "I feel the same way." Right next to the edge of a cliff. I felt a sense of foreboding, like there was something about to hit me, but I didn't know where it would come from. The same feeling you'd get if someone threw something at you from outside your vision. That strange moment when the incoming energy bends the air around you and then, *thwack*, you're beaned by a baseball to the temple.

Ariane returned with a photo album. She opened it and laid it in front of Sasha and me. Inside was a photo of a man holding a baby. "There's Dad holding Peter. Peter was three months old, I think?" Ariane smiled softly. "I can barely remember."

It was hard for me to focus on what she said. Instead, I couldn't stop staring at the man in the picture. It was Mr. Mueller. The same face. The same way of standing. Even the facial hair. This was the man whom I'd seen in person that morning, looking the same more than forty years ago.

Sasha and I had already started to embrace the idea that Mr. Mueller was, in fact, a ghost haunting Blackrock Glen, a ghost who had some power over the building's cockroaches. But here was the physical proof. That a man who'd done something so monstrous could appear the way he was in that picture—joyful while holding a smiling baby, a baby who would grow up to idolize the hatred inside Mueller— it knocked the wind out of me. I turned to Sasha, and she looked physically ill.

Sasha regained her composure first. "Could we use some of this?" she asked. "Would it be okay if we took some pictures?"

"Oh, feel free," Ariane said. Behind her, I swore I saw something dart down the wall. Something small and dark.

Something that reminded me a lot of a roach.

CHAPTER 25

THE SECOND WE'D GOTTEN BACK INTO THE car, I'd texted Al and Mom to get out of the building, but my messages were unread. I hoped that they weren't home. Maybe Al had gone into the city and Mom had a playdate set up for Gracie.

At 6:58 p.m. Yeah, sure, totally realistic expectation.

Sasha and I didn't speak until we were back on the highway.

"Holy crap," I said. "It's him."

"It's him," Sasha replied.

"I'm trying to understand this, and it's like trying to swallow a horse whole," I said. "None of this is supposed to happen. These things are stories. Stuff you tell little kids to get them to behave, but it ends up giving them nightmares. I mean, what does he want? What could a dead arsonist possibly want now?"

"He wouldn't have worked for Al if he simply wanted to burn the building down—he could have done that anytime. He was cool with the building . . . until he wasn't. He said the 'undesirables' made him realize his plan had to change, but what was his plan?"

I blinked. "What do ghosts usually want?"

"In the movies? Usually they want everyone out of their space, right? Like, get out or I make the walls bleed and turn your breakfast into maggots or whatever."

"Which would explain the roach infestations. He would use those as his way of keeping the building from ever opening."

Sasha's eyes widened. "Maybe." She held a hand up and shook her head. "But then he let you folks back in. He didn't extend the fumigation."

"The fumigation was actually shorter than they told us it'd be." But why? Mueller could have kept the building tented if he'd so desired.

"I know you don't want to, but try to remember what happened after you moved back in," Sasha said.

It wasn't hard to remember—it had been less than seventy-two hours ago. "The first night back, I had terrible nightmares. The next morning, you and I ran into each other, and then I offered to help Mueller and Peter. They told me to go to the ninth floor, but I went to ten. And that's where I saw Frankie get possessed." I tried to remember how things had played out from there. "Even though I was totally frantic about Frankie, it seemed like Mueller only cared that I'd gone to ten. Like, I wasn't supposed to see what was happening there."

"That's fucked up."

"It is. Mueller acted all pleased with himself, as if he had possessed Frankie for my benefit."

"What do you mean?"

"He was all, 'Isn't it nicer to get along' or some shit. Which brings us to today. It was right after Mueller learned about the affordable units that he said the plan needed to change. They found out the building's going to have tenants from all social classes, and *then* the plan changes." I clenched my eyes shut, thinking. "But what was the plan before, and what's the plan now? I have no idea what would be next."

"This is all ridiculous, right? Like, we're trying to rationalize the actions of a dead racist who killed himself while burning a building down."

I understood her reaction; I couldn't wrap my head around this either. Mueller was real. I'd stood next to him. I'd shaken his hand. There wasn't anything about him that seemed unnatural. He was just a simple old man. Even the racism, while wrong, felt like something a man his age would cling to. Why would a ghost bother with that kind of thing anymore? Wasn't death supposed to bring some peace?

Sasha broke the silence. "Manny, I'm not sure what we're supposed to do next. I don't know if the police or the Department of Housing handles these kinds of things."

"And we do?"

"Maybe we see a priest?"

"The priest always dies in these kinds of movies, Sasha."

Sasha thought on that. "We need to pause, then. We *are* dealing with a ghost and his crazy grandchild. I don't feel as if we talked about that enough, right? Like, a *ghost* ghost. This man died. We read about it. We had his daughter *tell* us about it."

I licked my lips; they were dry. "I feel like I should be more freaked out. Like, why aren't I freaked out that I was spending time with a dead man? That he put roaches inside me?" The thought wouldn't settle into place. Like a basketball spinning on the rim. I wanted it to go into the net, but it refused to.

"And his very alive, very large adult grandson," Sasha said.

"I think I saw a roach in Ariane's house too. It's like Mueller has this vast army of spies everywhere, all reporting back to the main hive."

"An undead dude and an army of roaches." Sasha shook her head in disbelief.

I felt parched. "I think the only one that has all the

answers is Mueller himself. But if he was willing to burn a building down because—"

"He's a racist, and I told you his ass was racist."

"You totally win that one. So, if he burned all these buildings down because of racism, then he must be doing whatever it is he's doing now for the same reason."

"For racism," Sasha said.

"For racism."

"And we're here cracking jokes while there's a possibility that this is all true, and I can't think of anyone who would believe or help us," Sasha said. She smirked. "Hell, if we called the cops, they'd team up with him."

"I mean, we have all your research. And now we have the photos you took of Mueller when he was young. Or rather, the same age, but from a long time ago. That must mean something. Someone would believe us, right?"

"I don't know, dude. I'm still having a hard time believing it, and I saw you vomit roaches."

The weight of defeat came in hot. I felt spiritually crushed. There were no answers for this that made any sense, and we were right: nobody was going to help us. "We can forget about this. End of the day, it's none of our business. Let him burn down the building. It's not like it's filled with people."

"Manny, it could still affect the block. It could still affect your family. How do we stop that?" Sasha gently tapped the steering wheel. "The last time that man burned a building down, it sent ripples. Maybe we don't see it, but I can imagine the impact he had. I mean, how often do fires go out of control? What if it spread down the block? What if that's his intention? We can't risk the well-being of people who aren't even involved."

"Then we save the folks we care about," I said. "And then we walk away and let the dead racist have what he wants, an empty building."

Sasha kept her eyes on the road. "You're getting scared." Not a question, a statement.

"I'm always scared." I felt a flutter in my stomach. "I mean, I'm willing to get Al, my mom, and the baby out of there, but I'm not sure I'm strong enough to deal with whatever comes out of confronting this head-on. We're just kids, Sasha."

"Then who else is going to do this?" She scoffed. "I know I hate Blackrock Glen for the long-term harm it's going to have on the neighborhood. But this man, I don't think he'll stop at an empty building. He's an immediate threat to all of us. I can't walk away knowing that if we figured out a way to stop him . . ."

"That it could do long-term good."

"Exactly." Sasha laughed. "Or we're talking out our asses because we're coping."

I stared out my window. "Do you really care about the

neighborhood like that, though? I feel like you and I both see bigger places for us out there."

"Okay, change of subject, but no. I do like it here. I'd be happy to take a train to NYU or Hunter or wherever and stay in my community." Sasha pulled a stick of gum from the center console. "I feel the fear thing, Manny, but I think we both need to accept that any version of what's next is scary."

"And it's only us."

"Maybe. But there's two of us. We got each other's backs, right?"

The feeling wouldn't leave me. It was a compulsion, a need to give this up. To abandon the plan and simply let things play out. I couldn't believe how ridiculous this still felt. A voice in my head seemed to scream, *Stop this. You know it's useless. People are in danger and if you were smart, Manny, you'd make sure your people weren't in the crosshairs.*

"Manny, are you still with me?"

"Uh, yeah." My head was swimming.

"You're looking green again. Do you think you got all the roaches out?"

"Jesus, yeah, Sasha. It's just so overwhelming, and all I want you to do is keep driving past our exit."

"You should be mad, though. He tried to use you. To what ends, we don't know yet, but he did, nonetheless. He violated you, Manny."

Sasha was right. I was jumping at shadows in my own head. Mueller had exploited me. He'd seen how vulnerable I'd been with the move and used that to try to make me into a monster, or at least fill me with monsters. Mueller had infested me and had made me a puppet for him. Was that what was behind those sudden moments of self-doubt and paranoid fear? Those feelings were with me before I met Mueller, but they had gone up to an eleven since I'd met him, hadn't they? Me throwing the bowl at Al. All that anger every time I was anywhere near the building. And now he had Frankie and who knew who else under his sway. I wanted to confront him, to fight him, but how could I do that? I was a regular kid, and this *thing* was something I was entirely unequipped to deal with.

I closed my eyes tight. There was a piercing pain in the center of my head. I wanted to go home and lie down, but I wasn't about to find peace at Blackrock Glen. "We can't keep waiting anymore."

"I agree," Sasha said. "But do we have any idea how to stop him?"

"Maybe those devices from before," I said. "The one at your apartment did something to me. If we get more, we could plug them in all over the building. Use them to drive the roaches out."

"And the one thing that Mueller can do—control the roaches—we take off the table."

"Exactly."

"But what if he figures it out and cuts the power in the building?"

Crap. I hadn't thought of that. I hadn't thought of a million things. I checked my phone and looked up the device and the sound it produced. "Maybe they have it recorded somewhere?" I did a quick search on YouTube. "I found a video that plays the sound."

"Dude, you really think it's legit? I mean, all we hear is a whole lot of nothing."

"We may as well have a backup?"

"I guess."

"What about the large adult grandson?"

"I guess we hit him?"

Sasha looked over to me. "Manny, have you ever actually fought anyone?"

"No. I can barely have an argument with anyone who isn't in my family, and even then, I suck at it." There it was, though. My family. I was brave enough to argue with my family, but I wasn't brave enough to save them?

We turned onto Blackrock Avenue and passed 243. Mueller's van wasn't in the driveway—good news.

"Crap, Manny." Sasha slapped my chest with the back of her hand.

The unwelcome news: the van was in front of Blackrock Glen. The worse news: Mueller was standing right there at the van's rear, staring at us as we drove closer. Sasha jammed on the brakes.

"He's looking right at us," she said.

I locked eyes with Mueller, and he sneered. He turned and grabbed a bottle from the back of the van and walked toward the building. He stopped and looked back at me—it was the look he'd given Sasha when they'd first met. His *real* face—the facade was gone.

I realized what the change in plan meant then. He couldn't get what he wanted, and the last time that happened . . .

The building and my family were in trouble.

Mueller disappeared into the building. I jumped out of the car to follow him.

"Manny!" Sasha called out. "We still need the stuff from Mueller's house."

I stopped in my tracks as Sasha pulled her car to the curb and stepped out. "I know you want to run in there, but we can't go in without something, and we know that something is in that man's backyard."

I nodded. Sasha was right. Even if I found a little bravery, I couldn't let that make me stupid. I'd get everyone killed that way. Everything I feared would come true. I crossed the street, and Sasha joined me.

"We'll be quick," she said.

We broke into a run toward Mueller's. Thankfully, the house was dark. "Doesn't look like anyone's home."

I stopped short at the end of the driveway. As I stood there, realizing the scope of everything, the terror set back in. The experiences that had led us here. The roaches—being covered and possessed by them. The outbursts and the arguments. The feeling of hopelessness that had gripped me since we'd first driven onto this block. All of it descended on me, and the twenty or thirty feet we had to walk to get to the trash cans might as well have been a leaping jump into the Grand Canyon in the dead of night.

Like Sasha said, though—this would be quick.

So why wouldn't my legs move?

Sasha sighed and went first. I hesitated and then finally followed, shame being a good motivator. We crouched down as we hustled to Mueller's backyard gate. The latch to open it was silent. We slowly swung it open and slipped into the backyard. The cans were where they'd been.

"Which one again?" Sasha whispered.

"The third from the right," I whispered back.

Sasha quickly grabbed the bag and pulled it from the can. Something clattered onto the concrete floor, and I remembered the stupid bag was torn open. Sasha froze as lights went on inside the house.

"Go, go, go." I motioned her toward the gate.

Sasha booked it as I lingered when I saw a figure silhouetted in the back door's glass pane. The moment's hesitation left me standing there as the outdoor light came on, and the door swung open. Peter emerged. He had a bottle of whiskey in one hand and a cigarette in the other. His eyes were wet, his face mottled with red patches. He stared at me, his eyes looking up and down and then over to the trash cans. The disdain was still there on his face, but he himself looked three sizes smaller. As if something had drained out of him.

Peter stayed at the doorway and wiped his eyes with the back of an arm before taking a puff of his cigarette. "Why are you here?" he slurred.

I straightened myself up as much as I could. The silence between us broke when my stomach churned. I clenched my fists and took the longest breath I'd ever taken in my life. I took stock of the situation. Peter wasn't with Mueller. He was here. He was drunk. He was crying. Something must have happened between them. If not, Peter would have been at Blackrock Glen with Mueller, getting ready to burn the building down.

Sasha stood at the foot of the driveway and motioned to me. "Manny, come on. Forget him."

I wanted to forget him, but I couldn't. I knew the pain in his eyes. That was loss. That was anger. I knew that look so well, and I thought that I might have the right idea of what I could do about it. I had to take the gamble. It was the only chance we had if these devices were a bust.

I stood my ground and swallowed. "We need to talk, Peter," I said. "We need to talk about everything."

CHAPTER 26

"WHAT DO YOU WANT?" PETER TOOK A long drink from his bottle and sat down on the top step of the stoop. It was strange to see him so loose. Every time I'd seen him before, it seemed like he'd had a curtain rod strapped to his back; he didn't look like a person who could ever bend. On that stoop, though, he looked barely capable of holding his shape. As if he'd melt down the steps at any second.

"You know why I'm here," I said. "And you've probably figured out that we know what your grandfather is." I took one step forward. "We need your help. We need to stop this before your grandfather does something worse."

Peter shook his head and stared into the distance. "You can't stop him."

"See? This is a waste of time," Sasha said. "Screw roach racist junior over here, and let's go."

I held a hand up. I needed a minute. "Please, Peter. We have those gadgets, but I don't think they're gonna be enough. Maybe for the roaches, but not for the man . . . or whatever he is now."

"I found him, you know. I . . . I was going to burn down Blackrock Glen when they were starting to build it. I wanted . . ." Peter closed his eyes. "I had the same urges he did. So, when they said they were putting up a new building, I thought I'd do something in his memory. We were so much alike. My mom used to say it all the time—'You have his eyes' in nice moments, or 'You have his temper' in bad ones." He clicked his tongue against his teeth. "And then this miracle happens. There he was, this man I dreamed about meeting for so long."

"You don't have to be like him, though. Just because your hair parts the same or you laugh the same doesn't mean you have to let this happen, Peter," I said. "I mean, I don't know you, but you don't come off like the type of person who wants people to die."

"What the hell do you know about me?" Peter scrunched up his face. "You're the worst of this. You came along, and he got all obsessed with you. You had the 'right kind of anger,' he said." He snorted. "Texas brat that don't even look Puerto Rican. It was like you were an ideal to him. I had my grandfather back for a minute, and along you came. It was like I didn't exist."

"Dude, he possessed me with roaches. Are you jealous of that?"

Peter took another drink. "You *meant* something to him. Me? I was his henchman. And then once I wasn't cool with one frigging thing, he dumped me." He made an arc with his smoking arm. "My ma called me today for the first time in months, and he tells me that I'm weak, that my conviction is gone." Peter sniffed. "He told me I'm sick. Did you know that? That I . . . that the roaches felt it. I'm dying, Manny. All these fuckin' chemicals." He gave a sad laugh. "The roaches knew they couldn't control me without killing me like they killed the others." He stared down at his feet. "I told my mother. I told her I was sick, and when I did . . ." Peter choked back a sob. "When I did, she told me she loved me and for me to go to her house and I . . . I don't know, I felt stupid. Wasting my time with a dead man. Trying to do what he wanted while I know I won't get the same chance as him. Once I'm gone, I'm *gone*. I told him I couldn't do this anymore. I was done."

"You wanted to go to her."

Peter nodded. "He said I was abandoning him, and then he abandoned me. As if I was a stranger."

"You did a lot for him. I get that," I said. I knew I didn't have time to listen to Peter's feelings, but I felt like he was on the verge of helping us.

Peter scoffed. "It didn't have to come to this. Did you know that we faked the fumigation? We even carted in old chemicals to make it all look legit. We were just going to draw it out forever. Leave those tents up long enough to get the building in trouble or even abandoned. Then it finally clicked in Opa's head who Blackrock Glen was for—there weren't a lot of luxury condos in the Bronx back in his day— and he changed his mind. He liked the idea of the neighborhood getting richer."

"You mean whiter," Sasha noted.

Peter pointed at Sasha. "But you and your petition." Then he pointed at me. "And you going where you weren't supposed to. It all came crashing down."

I looked at Sasha, and she met my gaze. My gut was right. Mueller didn't get his way, and now he was going to burn it all down again. Something Peter had said earlier stood out.

"You mentioned others—are you saying he possessed people other than me and Frankie?"

"Killed them, more like. Nobody survived that crap until you. That anger inside you, all that negative energy, it must have given you a leg up. Opa said it was the same as what was inside him."

My cheeks burned with shame.

Peter shrugged. "Either way, as soon as he got you, he got all moony about your ass. Acted like you were a kindred spirit." He frowned. "I told him you were just another

teenage asshole, that this neighborhood already had plenty
of those. I mean, look at that thug he took."

Frankie. Was the possession going to kill Frankie?

"Peter, is Frankie with Mueller?"

"Who cares, man?" Peter threw his hands up, and the
bottle of whiskey flew into the air. He stumbled to catch it
and missed, and the bottle shattered on the pavement. He
hung his head. "Man, I'm dying. Why should I care about
any of this anymore? Like I said, I'm not going to do the
deed."

Peter was giving up. And could I really blame him? His
dead grandfather had tossed him aside with a death sen-
tence. It had to hurt. Still, that same dead grandfather was
also a manipulative asshole. He'd taken advantage of all my
weaknesses. It wasn't crazy to believe he'd done the same
to Peter.

"Dude, how are you so sure you're dying? Because
Mueller said so? What if he's messing with your head to
control you? I mean, you *idolized* him, Peter," I said. "You
don't think he could have taken advantage of that like he
did with me? He used you until he was done with you and
then threw you out."

Peter blinked. "But we're family. I had this chance to be
with him, and all he did was choose to focus on everything
else *but* me. All he gave me was a goddamn diagnosis." He
laughed cruelly and lowered his head. "Ma was right. I need

to go to her place. I came here, and all it did was make me more miserable than I ever was."

I couldn't wait any longer. "Look, man, I really wish we could stand here and debate all day, but I've got a baby sister, and your grandfather is going to get her killed. If you really wanted to show that asshole who you were, you'd stand up and help me. I get that you have whatever issues you have, but is it wrong of me to assume a dead kid is something you're not cool with?"

Peter sighed and shook his head. "I was only in this to scare people out of there. That was it. People dying? I wasn't in this for that. I just figured I'd have fun with the old man."

"This stopped being a game a long time ago, Peter. Your grandfather is after my family now. They're in danger."

"You're the one he wants, but yeah, after all this, it's entirely possible he'll do something to them to get to you."

"Then help me, Peter. Please. I'm begging you."

Peter put out his cigarette. "He's going to kill us all, you realize that?"

"Well, you said you were already dying," I said. "Why not die a hero?"

Peter stood up and wiped his hands on his pants. "Those sonic pest repellents worked on you?"

I nodded.

"Well, shit, first time for everything." Peter came down the stairs. "Fine. This is all my fault either way."

"Awesome, great—let's get a move on, please." Sasha motioned for us to join her.

Peter walked past me and stopped. "I'm sorry, by the way."

"Don't be sorry—help us," I said. "Help us make this right."

"I don't know what makes it right. I think he doesn't go away until he's finished with what he's finally decided to do," Peter said.

"And what's that?"

"Burn that place to the ground."

If that was true, if the only way to stop Mueller was to let the building burn, I was fine with that. What mattered was that I stopped him from hurting anybody else. Personally, I thought there had to be more to all of this. Mueller had had plenty of chances to burn down Blackrock Glen long before my family and I had arrived. That he was finally moving now made me think there was more to his motives. Maybe he hadn't wanted to be the one to light the fire. Maybe he'd intended it to be me but couldn't work out exactly how to get me to do it. I wanted to believe we had a chance to prevent anything bad from happening, but at the same time, it felt inevitable.

If Blackrock Glen burned, I had to make sure only Mueller burned with it.

CHAPTER 27

WE RAN. ME IN FRONT, PETER NEXT, AND Sasha behind. Blackrock Glen was completely dark, save for one apartment on the fourteenth floor—my home. It was as if Mueller was beckoning me. I pointed out the lit windows to the others, and they nodded. The fear didn't really set in again until I was a foot from the entrance of Blackrock Glen. The lobby was empty, but something felt wrong.

"I'm about ready to start praying out loud, Manny." Sasha pushed Peter to the side and peeked inside too. "It looks safe, right?"

"It's definitely not safe," Peter said. "My grandfather wants you in there."

"What do you mean?" Sasha asked. "Why would he want us in there?"

Peter looked at her as if she were stupid. "He's angry. And he wants to exact revenge on the people who have gotten in his way. That includes the two of you."

"Are you saying what I think you're saying? He wants us in the building when he burns it down?" Sasha shuddered.

"What do you suggest we do?" I asked Peter.

"Go up there, but don't take the elevators—you don't want to be in a confined space in that building. Roaches will be on you in a matter of seconds."

"So, we take the stairs," Sasha said.

"At least we can run if we have to." I turned to Peter. "Do you think he's possessed anyone else?"

"He definitely has," Peter said, "but I don't know if any of them survived. Opa didn't really understand how to control the roaches at first, and they sort of . . ." He trailed off.

"Sort of what?" Sasha asked, though I didn't think either of us wanted the answer.

"They sort of ate the bodies from the inside out."

I was going to be sick.

"Once he got better at controlling them, he was able to prolong the process. I mean, everybody still died, just not as fast."

That was not comforting.

"You and Frankie were the last two people I knew that he had possessed. But that doesn't mean he hasn't gotten to others. You're lucky you purged the roaches when you did.

All that teenage angst of yours was keeping you safe since the roaches fed off that anger, but it couldn't have lasted forever. You need to save your buddy as soon as you can. He doesn't have your . . . constitution." Peter perked his head up and stared into the building. "That said, I have no idea what else my grandfather might be capable of."

Awesome. At least there had been one positive to all the anger I'd felt about moving. I put my key into the front-door lock and turned. The lock engaging was louder than I expected, and opening the door seemed even more deafening. Inside, I only heard the buzzing of lights. We walked through the second door, and that was when I heard the clicking.

"The hell is that?" Sasha asked.

"Just go to the stairs," Peter said.

We walked to the stairs quickly, but I stopped as the lights above began to flicker.

"He knows we're here," I said.

Down the hall, a shadow grew from around the corner. The shape skittered into view, lurching forward, the light bouncing off their face.

Frankie.

He roared and rushed toward us. He was impossibly fast, and before I knew it, he was leaping on me and wrapping his hands around my neck. His eyes were bulging out of their sockets, and his skin was covered in blisters and scabs. I could see his flesh moving as the roaches crawled beneath his skin. I felt the roaches moving in his fingers as he strangled me. He brought his face over mine and opened his mouth wide enough for me to see the shining carapaces of the roaches lining his throat and mouth. He was infested.

Peter came up from behind and tried pulling Frankie off me.

Frankie growled as he turned to look at Peter. "Traitor," he yelled.

I continued to grapple with Frankie, turning my head side to side to shake the roaches off my face. I caught a glimpse of Sasha; she was reaching under a table in the hallway and unplugging a table lamp. "Hold him off one more second," she said as she plugged one of the sonic emitters into an outlet.

I saw the twitch in Frankie's face and the change in his eyes. I knew what was coming next, so I turned my head as far to one side as I could. Thankfully, his grip loosened, and I was able to roll out from under him as he unleashed a torrent of bile and roaches. I scrambled to my feet, as did Peter, and watched as Frankie purged his system.

I backed up from the mess. Frankie grabbed at his throat as he continued retching and, once done, collapsed to the ground, exhausted and bleeding.

Sasha ran over and checked on him. "He's breathing, but they messed him up bad," she said as she turned to face us. "How could you let him do this to people?" she asked Peter.

Peter didn't have an answer. He slowly looked away with shame in his eyes. "It shouldn't have been like this."

Sasha grabbed her phone. "He needs an ambulance," she said.

I nodded. "Get him outside and call for help."

Sasha stood up and hugged me. "Be careful. Don't do anything too stupid, like dying."

"I'll try." I hugged her back. "I'm sorry I sucked as a friend. I probably could have been a lot better at this."

"Eh, you're fine. Once we get out of this, I'll give you a list of things to work on." Sasha looked at Peter with rage in her eyes. "And you . . ."

Peter raised his hands. "Hey, I know. I'm here to help. I swear."

"Yeah, well, I don't believe you." She pointed to me. "Manny, keep him in front of you."

"I got it."

"There's that old roach spray we brought in and other supplies on the third floor," Peter said. "We can stop there and get more in case these devices don't work."

I eyed him. "Is it real roach spray?"

"Yes. We kept a bunch of crap we never used lying around to pretend like we were working."

I pocketed as many of the sonic devices as I could and

passed some to Peter. "Okay. Let's go to the third floor. Plug these in. We get the spray, and then we go upstairs."

The plan was set, and there was no time to waste. Peter and I ran to Stairwell A. I kept him in front of me—Sasha was right; there was no way to know whether he was entirely trustworthy or if he would have another change of heart if he encountered his grandfather on the way upstairs.

Peter swung open the door to the stairs, and my choice to keep him in front paid off almost immediately. Before we made it up the second flight, someone leapt on him. Peter fell back and collided with me, taking me down along with him. I scrambled to my feet to see Peter struggling with a man I'd never seen before. He was dressed in drab overalls, his hair hanging over his face in thick, wet strands. The man was trying to strangle Peter.

"Trai . . . tor . . . ," the man rasped.

I grabbed the man's shoulders and pulled. He flew backward—I guess I didn't know my own strength—but as soon as he landed, he stood back up with unnatural speed. Now that he was standing, I got a better look at him. The man wasn't right. He looked gray. He reached his hands out toward Peter, ignoring me. They were missing fingernails, the tips of his fingers gummed and red. The man opened his mouth, and roaches crawled out up into his nose and into his empty eye sockets.

The sight sent me over the edge, and I kicked at the man

as hard as I could, but instead of feeling a solid hit, it was as if I were kicking a bag of leaves. The man's midsection caved in, and more roaches poured out of him. He couldn't stand straight anymore but managed to stay on his feet.

"The hell is this?" I said.

"I think Opa's pissed off at me for helping you." Peter spit. "Let's keep moving."

We ran up the stairs and reached the second-floor landing before two more like the man downstairs showed up. Peter shoved one to the side, and the man tumbled over the rail and burst open as he hit the ground. Thousands of roaches flowed out of him and started climbing the walls back toward us.

"It's the contractors," Peter said. "The ones he possessed first."

This was the result of Mueller's possession? This was what he had been willing to do to me so he could make me do what he wanted? These people were hollowed out, skin puppets driven by the roaches Mueller controlled. Peter punched another possessed man, and the thing's face caved in with a dry crunch. They were cardboard people, no longer human. The roaches had eaten everything inside them and left them husks.

With both attackers broken, Peter and I ran up to the third floor and found the apartment with roach spray and masks.

Peter handed me a bottle of the spray. It was about the size and weight of a gallon of water and had a tube and nozzle attached to it. "Just point and pull the trigger," he said. "And here, put one of these on." He passed a mask to me, and I slipped it on. Peter then picked up a bottle and mask for himself.

We went back into the hallway and headed for the stairs. "Plug in one of those things by the stairwell," he said. "It'll help keep anyone from following us upstairs."

I did as I was directed and plugged one of the devices in near the door at the stairwell. Peter and I continued up, both of us moving slower than before. My legs and chest were on fire, and I was sure that drinking all that whiskey earlier wasn't doing Peter any favors. He stopped to dry heave, holding the back of a shaking hand up to his mouth and waving me off with the other.

"I'm fine," he said. "Keep moving."

On the ninth floor, the lights finally went out. I turned in place, my heart dropping into my stomach. The air felt thin.

"Shit," Peter muttered.

I blinked, trying to get my eyes to adjust to the dark. "There's supposed to be backups," I said.

"Maybe he cut those off."

I heard shambling. "Be careful. You're going to fall."

"What are you talking about?" Peter asked.

"I'm saying to take it slow, or we'll both fall."

"I'm not moving."

The emergency lights flickered on, a pale yellow engulf-ing us. Standing right in front of me was another of Mueller's victims. I screamed and leapt backward as it grabbed me by my shirt collar. We tumbled down a flight of stairs, twisting as we fell before slamming onto the landing below. I landed on top of the creature—it was no longer human—and its body flattened under my weight, causing hundreds of roaches to appear. They crawled all over me. I jumped up and swiped my arms and legs in a panic.

Peter was busy with another set of puppets. They were in worse shape than any of the others we'd seen thus far. The skin on their hands and faces had completely ripped open, making the roaches inside clear as day, congregating on exposed bone and rotting muscle. Thick, brown fluid leaked from the open wounds. It smelled like rotted fruit.

I turned to head back up the stairs but was grabbed by another one. It was like a walking skeleton, its loose clothes barely hanging on to its frame. The puppet wore a company-branded jacket with a name tag on it—MELVIN. Al's prede-cessor. Had Mueller really been working that long at using this power of his?

I shoved Melvin into the crowd that Peter was battling, and a few of the puppets burst open. The roaches inside them were larger than the little brown ones that had been haunt-ing me since I'd arrived at Blackrock Glen. These looked engorged. As they fell to the floor, they began to scamper toward Peter and me, their antennae pointed at us and their very visible mandibles opening and closing manically.

Peter started to spray the growing wave of angry roaches as he climbed the stairs backward. "Go up," he said.

I stomped on some of the roaches and raced up the stairs. The way was clear, but for how long, who knew? It was impossible to know what was waiting for me, but I had to get there.

On the twelfth floor, there was a loud bang below us as the door to the eleventh nearly flew off its hinges. A dozen or more "people" came through the threshold. These had to be all the contractors that Al had complained about, the ones who hadn't shown up for work. But they had, only Mr. Mueller had gotten to them first. Folks simply trying to do their jobs had been possessed by Mueller, drunk on his power or, at least, testing the limits of it.

Peter stopped. "Get upstairs, kid. Just go. I'll keep them busy."

"We're right here. They can't catch up with us."

Peter shook his head. "No. We can't risk it. One of us has to stop him."

The first new puppet came closer. Peter kicked it in the head, and it stumbled down the stairs, roaches erupting from various parts of its body. The roaches were even fatter than the ones possessing the bodies in the stairwell—clearly, feasting on their hosts' innards had helped them grow. They seemed to be faster, too—they raced right back up the stairs and started climbing up Peter's leg. He shook a few off and swatted away some others, then sprayed them. The roaches twitched and died, but there were plenty more where those came from.

"Get the hell out of here," Peter screamed as one of the bigger roaches—the size of my palm—crawled onto his face and bit his cheek. Peter tore it off, a sizable piece of skin going with it.

I lingered at the top of the flight. I'd come here to keep people from dying, not to sacrifice someone. It didn't matter if Peter was or wasn't on his grandfather's side; he didn't deserve to die.

"No." I grabbed Peter by the arm and pulled him up the stairs, turning to spray at roaches still coming after him. He did his part too, kicking the next puppet down the stairs and yanking more roaches off his hands. I looked down the stairs. The roaches from the other bodies were gaining on us. The stairs farther down looked to be covered in inky water flowing in the wrong direction. Mueller had called on his entire army—they were after us, and they were not going to stop.

We continued fighting until we got to the next-to-last flight before the fourteenth floor. There were roaches everywhere, scrambling up the stairs as fast as we were moving.

I sprayed near my feet and nearly slipped. The poison was potent enough to make me dizzy despite the mask I was wearing, but some of the roaches weren't even flinching.

One of the contractors grabbed at Peter's ankle, and Peter went down hard. He quickly rolled onto his back and kicked at the puppet, but it was able to hold on. The creature crawled up Peter's body, and once they were face-to-face, it opened its mouth, and a stream of roaches poured out and covered Peter from chin to chest. He screamed as the roaches tore at his clothes and bit his flesh. Peter forced the monster off him, though he stumbled down a few steps, the roaches and other puppets overtaking him.

"No!" I went to grab Peter, but he pushed me away and locked his eyes with mine. "No. Go save them. Stop that man. You stop that man, okay?"

Our breathing matched. The world stood still. "I . . . I don't know . . ."

"You can do this, Manny. I know it. I screwed it all up, and I'm sorry. . . ."

The puppets pulled at Peter again. The roaches stopped swarming toward me and turned all their attention to Peter—the traitor had to pay. Peter gritted his teeth and turned, throwing a wild haymaker at the nearest roach zombie. Its head exploded, and roaches covered the walls. The exposed roaches and remaining roach zombies came back at Peter in a fervor. More joined in, and Peter disappeared into the group. He screamed, and I saw his hands rise above the zombies' heads and drive back down. He wasn't going to give up.

"Manny, run!" he called out.

Mueller was sending me a clear message: *Look at what I'll do to my own family. Imagine what I'll do to yours.*

I ran and careened onto the fourteenth floor.

CHAPTER 28

I PULLED THE DOOR TO THE STAIRWELL shut behind me, tearing my mask off. The lights above me flickered, making the hallway creepy AF. Thankfully, the hall was clear, not that it would stay that way. I activated a device and moved farther down the hall, plugging one into every socket I passed. It was quiet, too quiet. No puppets. No roaches. Things weren't okay, though. I had watched Peter get dragged away. I wasn't sure he was dead, but I didn't doubt Mueller would kill him.

I wasn't dealing with a man. I was dealing with a monster.

When I got to our apartment, I tested the door—locked. I dug into my pants for my keys. My hands were shaking so bad, I could barely get the key into the lock, but I finally got it on the fifth try. I was out of sonic devices, so before I opened the door, I started the YouTube video I'd found earlier.

I entered the apartment. It was now dark, save for the ambient light coming in through the windows. I could see that the kitchen and living room were empty. I crept to my parents' room—no one. I flipped some switches, and the apartment filled with light.

"Al! Ma!" I called out. "Gracie?"

No answer.

Oh god, please. "Ma!" Nobody was here. Why was nobody here?

I didn't know what else to do. Where were they? I checked my phone. Still no response to my texts to Mom and Al. I texted Sasha.

In my apartment. No one here.

Police and EMTs here, she wrote back immediately. U ok?

"I would not recommend staring at your phone at a time like this."

I almost jumped out of my skin. The voice was low and weak. Unfamiliar. It had come from the living room.

I walked back to the front of the apartment. I turned on the overhead lights and found a zombie sitting in the middle of the floor, surrounded by Gracie's toys. He gave me a crooked smile, and a roach crept out of his mouth, up his jawline, and into his ear. My video wasn't having an effect, so that was a bust. I cut it off and stuffed my phone into my pocket.

"You can talk through them now?" I kept my distance.

"This was what I liked most about you, Manuel. Your intelligence. You are so much better than the people of this place, yet you do not realize that. Your kindness and your conscience, they do you no favors. They make you so weak." The body leaned forward a moment and then sat straight. "It has taken so much practice to get this strong. I still have moments of . . . weakness, I suppose." The corpse forced a smile. Roaches crawled between the gaps in his teeth. "Practice makes perfect. Soon enough, these puppets will do everything I need of them. Soon *you* will do what I ask of you too."

I shook my head. "You're acting like I was important to whatever it is you want to do here, but you could have burned this place down whenever you wanted. You had a million chances. Instead, you did this." I pointed to the corpse in my living room. "Who is this? Why are you doing this?"

"This? This was the building inspector your stepfather has been waiting to hear from." The body spasmed. Its head hung low and then jerked back upward. "And your stepfather would have, unfortunately—the inspector discovered remnants of the infestation. I thought I'd hidden all of it. He found some. You did as well. I am learning so much."

"I know what you're going to do now. Peter told me."

"That is your fault. . . ." Mueller trailed off. "Your friend, she ruined it. Her efforts would sully what would have been a reclamation for this neighborhood—a return to when it was a good place to live. To raise a family."

It hit me. "So, burning this place down is how you take your ball and go home."

No answer.

I began to circle Mueller's surrogate but kept my distance. "Just let us go. You'll have the empty building. You can be here by yourself. Well, you and your roaches. You don't need to burn the building down. Nobody will bother you. Isn't that what you want?"

"I did, at first."

"Then what is it you want from me? What do I have to do to make you let my family go?"

"You betrayed me." The corpse shook his head. "I no longer want to be *alone*." He sneered, the dry skin cracking under the pressure of making the atrophied muscles move. "I want vengeance. I want you to suffer as I have."

I stepped away from him. That last word had impact, volume. He was furious with me. The anger was entirely based on his delusions, but that didn't make it less dangerous. "Then let them go, and I'll burn this place for you. You can have me. I'm the one you're mad at, not my family. They did nothing wrong. My sister's a baby—why would you hurt a baby?"

Mueller's proxy twitched. Some roaches broke through the flesh of his neck and fell to the ground. They crawled onto one of Gracie's teething rings.

"You stand there and offer what I want. You believe that if you make it easy, I would be tempted, but I do not trust you."

"I mean it," I said. "You want me to do this for you? Fine. I'm not going to let my family suffer because of anything I've done."

The proxy remained silent again.

"This is the only chance you get," I said. It was risky to give him the ultimatum, but I had to convince him to let my family out of here. I didn't care what happened to me. All that mattered was that they made it out of this alive.

The corpse laughed. "You're afraid, aren't you?"

He was toying with me, enjoying the little back-and-forth too much.

"I'm shitting my pants, Mr. Mueller, but I'll do whatever you want. Please let them go."

The corpse eyed me.

Slowly the proxy stood. It walked toward me. I backed away but found the wall behind me.

It leaned forward. "No. All of you will die." Then he lunged at me, grabbing me by the throat with surprising strength. The other puppets weren't this strong, but the building inspector had only been possessed a couple of days earlier. I pushed back and felt the bones in the proxy's chest start to collapse. Roaches crawled through the flesh and started to bite my hands.

Suddenly the corpse's head burst open as the wooden

piece of Gracie's tower-stacking toy pierced it. Goo and blood splashed onto my face, as did a few cockroaches, which I swatted away.

Sasha stood in the center of the living room staring down at the body, holding a rucksack in one hand.

"Holy shit, Sasha. Thank God."

"Did I just kill him?" she asked with panic in her eyes.

"No, no," I said. "He was already dead."

She breathed a sigh of relief. "You, uh, have something on your face," she said.

I reached up to my cheek and felt wetness. I raced to the bathroom to rinse the building inspector's remains off. I ran the water as hot as I could and scrubbed my hands and face. I looked in the mirror and barely recognized myself—there were dark circles around my eyes, and my skin was paler than I'd ever seen it. My hands started to tremble as the adrenaline faded.

Back in the living room, Sasha was crouching by the body. She pulled a wallet out of his back pocket. She looked through it. "James Harris."

"He's a building inspector. Was." Another innocent life lost to this madman.

"And your family?"

"Not here. I think this has all been a game for him. He made me come up here and watched me beg for my family, but he doesn't care."

"Then where is he? Where is everyone?"

It struck me. It was stupidly obvious. I started walking to the door but turned around. "Wait a sec, how did you get up here?"

"I came up Stairwell B." She held up the rucksack. "I found a bunch of stuff on the third floor. I thought we could use it."

"Nobody came after you?"

"Thankfully, no. Manny, where's Peter?" Sasha asked.

I shook my head. "I need to go."

"I'm coming with you. Where are we going?"

"Where else would the biggest roach in this goddamn building be?" I asked. "The basement."

CHAPTER 29

"THE BASEMENT?!" SASHA GRABBED MY shoulder from behind. "Manny, you know only bad shit happens in basements."

I turned around. "I know. But it must be where my family is," I said.

"Whatever. Just not alone." She grabbed me by the hand and led me toward Stairwell B.

"What about Frankie?" I asked her.

"Ambulance took him. I told them he had some sort of weird allergy attack and gave them his parents' info."

"You tell them anything else?"

Sasha shrugged. "What was I supposed to say? 'Also, there seems to be a roach problem inside. Actually, not really a roach problem, but a dead-man-who-can-control-roaches problem. Would you mind checking it out?'"

She wasn't wrong.

"I really wanted them to stay, especially when you didn't respond to my text." She paused. "I was really scared for you, Manny."

I squeezed her hand. "I'm okay," I told her. "It's for the best. There are roaches everywhere—Mueller would have just taken control of their bodies, and then we'd be battling zombies with guns."

We started descending the stairs. After a few flights, Sasha stopped.

"What are we doing?" she asked.

"What do you mean? We're going to the basement to stop that lunatic."

"How do we even do that, Manny?"

I didn't have time to think through a plan. "Sasha, my mother, my sister, and my father are going to die if I don't do something. I have to try. Mueller's a monster. He's an insane bigot who stopped caring about hurting people forty years ago, when he lit the last place up."

Sasha smiled sheepishly. "I hate that I agree with you."

I took her hands. "Sasha, you don't have to come with me. I don't *want* you to come with me. I couldn't take it if anything happened to you."

"Dude, I'm coming. I love the Bronx, and even if I don't necessarily love this building, I'm not going to stand around while some psychopath attacks my home." She handed me the rucksack she'd brought with her. "Good thing we have some extra supplies."

"Good thing," I said. "Then we head downstairs, kick Mueller's ass, and get my family out of here."

"You make it sound easy."

"I know."

We continued down the stairs in silence. I was terrified. I thought it wouldn't feel this way, that making the brave decision would somehow fill me up with courage, but that wasn't happening. I was scared, and that fear wouldn't go away. The way my heart dropped with every floor we descended.

But it didn't matter, did it? I knew what I had to do, and I knew that I was the one to do it. I was fortunate to have Sasha with me. She was a good friend. If I made it through this, I would make it up to her. I would call Clarissa and tell her I was sorry for being so disconnected too. I had let all these negative emotions run my life, and I had suffered the consequences. Now I was ready for a clean start. If I didn't stop Mueller, I might not get the chance to take a different path. No matter what, he wouldn't make me the worst version of myself again.

We got to the basement, and once I opened the door, I felt regret.

The walls were alive—literally. There was no way to tell

how many roaches were down there. They covered every surface. I had complained about their silence, but with this many moving, I could hear their legs clicking against each other's carapaces. It sounded like Rice Krispies in milk. There was a strong, nutty smell in the air. It was faint and old, like something left behind days ago. I noticed balloons hanging from the ceiling in rows of three; they looked like they were filled with clear liquid. I caught a whiff of something sharp—chemical—in the air too.

"Look," I said, and pointed to the balloons.

"This is super, super messed up." Sasha gingerly stepped into the basement, staring up. "He's got the place rigged up to burn."

I knelt and went through the rucksack Sasha had brought with her. There were a few heavy-duty painter's respirators— better than the masks from before. I put one on hastily and handed another to Sasha, before stuffing the extras into my bag—there was a good chance Al, Mom, and the baby would need them. Then I grabbed a can of roach fumigator, one of those deals where you set the can and let it emit a thick, heavy cloud of pesticide. I placed it down and set it off. Sasha put on her respirator and nodded at me.

The roach bomb was effective. Roaches began to fall off the walls and ceiling, landing on their backs, their legs moving as if they were sprinting toward nowhere. After a few seconds, the movement ceased, and the roaches lay still, like the husks of the people that Mueller had killed through possession.

We walked down the hall—I was leading us toward the old boiler room where I'd first met Mueller days before.

I set off a second roach bomb in the hall.

Sasha and I inched forward as the corpses of roaches rained down on us. I led her into the boiler room. I expected to find Mueller there, but there was no trace of him. There were a handful of balloons attached to the ceiling. At the opposite side of the boiler room, the wall was gone. Remnants of it littered the floor. We crossed the room, clinging to each other, and found concrete stairs leading down into pitch blackness. I turned on the flashlight on my phone. I was about to take a step down but stopped short.

"Jesus!" I yelped as I leapt backward. Someone was seated on the first stair, out of view. I flashed my light on him. Dead. There were more bodies on the steps past him. All splayed out in different poses. All of them with pieces missing. As if something had snacked on them for a little while and then moved on.

Sasha sidled up next to me. "Oh my god," she said.

"You think these are more contractors?" I asked. "Maybe the first people Mueller came into contact with?"

Sasha frowned. "Maybe. All these people . . . I just . . . Do people here not care when others go missing?" She looked at me.

I took a long breath. I was scared out of my mind, but knowing my family was down those stairs made me feel like I had to continue down into the darkness.

"Are you still good to keep going?" I asked.

"No." Sasha let out a small chuckle. "But we're going to, aren't we?"

"I think so."

I paced outside the new stairwell, trying to find some courage. I smacked my face a few times. I *had* to save them. This was bigger than our arguments. Through all the bullshit, my parents had stood by and supported me however they could—Al especially, in his own way. He'd taken the verbal beatings from me. He did all of that so Gracie, Mom, and I would be taken care of. He wasn't necessarily awesome at it sometimes, but I wasn't that awesome at being a part of my family either. Like him or not, Al was a good man, and he was a good dad. If we made it through this, I would tell him that. I would tell him that he did mean something to me. That I was grateful.

I had a lot of things to take care of once we got out of this, I thought, so I had to make sure I survived.

I set off a third roach bomb, and the sound of the roaches' hard bodies hitting the ground filled the room.

Sasha shined her phone's light down the stairs. "That's not helpful."

I pointed my flashlight in the same direction. There was

nothing for the light to reflect off, so all the damn thing did was let us know how much more darkness there was ahead of us. I closed my eyes and collected myself.

"A step at a time, right?" I asked.

"I guess." Sasha grabbed my free hand. "Together?"

I nodded. "Together."

We moved forward, and my heart pounded from the get-go. I increased my grip on Sasha's hand, and she reassuringly did the same. She didn't need to be here with me. As we descended, I could sense movement all around us, as if the roaches were escorting us to our destination. It felt like we were being watched, that same feeling I had had so many times before. Mueller's little spies alerting him that we were on our way.

"You're a good friend," I blurted out.

"Manny, this is the worst time to say something like that." Sasha was serious.

"I know. I know. I'm sorry."

"You're a good friend too. Even if you can be a dummy."

The descent wasn't too bad, but there was no rail, and the steps felt shorter than normal steps. I slipped a little, but Sasha helped me keep my footing.

"This must be the old basement," she said. "Of the building he burned down. The one that killed him."

I checked my phone for a signal. Two bars. 3G. Not great. The farther down we went, the more inevitable it was we'd lose reception completely. I had half a mind to tell Sasha to stay behind, but after everything we'd gone through, there was no way in hell she'd agree. I wouldn't either.

Besides, it felt much safer walking down those stairs hand in hand.

After the first flight, there was a tight turn leading to another flight. Down those stairs, another flight. How deep did this go down? The air felt weird; *I* felt weird. Like something was closing in on me, like I didn't have enough room around me. I reached my hands out and touched the walls.

"Does it feel tighter here?" I asked.

Sasha shifted uncomfortably. "I thought it was me," she said.

"Be careful."

"Oh, I am being very careful."

We kept going down. Each footfall sounding louder than the last.

"I keep wanting to talk," I said, "but I got nothing to say."

"Me too." Sasha nearly slipped, and I caught her. "I wish I had jokes."

No jokes. No words. Every step was closer to something we both dreaded. We made it down that flight of stairs and found a door. It looked old, but it was strangely clean. The hinges reflected light from our flashlights, and its hardware looked a lot like the door hardware we used upstairs.

"This is weird," Sasha said.

"You ready?" I asked.

"Nope."

We both reached for the door handle just as it engaged on its own, the door swinging away from us as if it was being opened by a ghost. I heard Sasha gasp next to me. There wasn't time to shine a light on the door before something came bounding toward us.

I pulled Sasha behind me, holding my flashlight in front of me like a bludgeon. A hand shot out of the darkness and grabbed me by the wrist. Sasha screamed.

It was Al.

Beat up, worse for wear, but it was Al.

"Manny?" His voice trembled. He held his hand up to shield his eyes, and I realized my flashlight was pointed right at his face. "What are you doing down here? We've got to get you out of here. Mr. Mueller, he's not who he says he is—"

Seeing him there, it did something to me. Made all the emotions boil up inside me. I snatched my mask off and collapsed against Al. I buried my head into his shoulder. "Dad," I cried. "Oh my god, you're okay."

Al rubbed my back but then pushed me away. He grabbed my shoulders as he gave me a once-over.

"Where's Mom? Where's Gracie?" I asked.

"He told me to get you where you needed to be, or he'd hurt them." Al's voice was strained. "I don't understand what that man is, Manny, but he's dangerous. The roaches—"

"I know," I said. "He wants me to burn this place down with all of us in it."

"Holy shit," Al said, running his hands through his hair. "Then we gotta get your mother and Gracie out of here." Al's demeanor flipped, the confusion and fear wiped away. "Did you two bring weapons? Anything we could use?"

"Sasha and I can distract him. Once you have a chance, you grab Gracie and Mom and you run. We'll be right behind you. I think he's dead set on having us here for the fire, so if we can get away from him as fast as we can, maybe it'll keep that from happening."

Al nodded slowly. "That sounds like a big gamble."

"I got nothing else," I said. "I just want to make sure you all get out of here."

"And you too, right?" Al asked.

I ignored the question. My legs were wobbly again, but I fought the urge to fall over. "Okay. Let's go."

Al led the way as we walked down a hallway that took us to a larger room. It reminded me of the basement upstairs except older and dingier. The walls were falling apart. Thick wads of cobwebs were everywhere, stretching from the ceiling to the walls. It smelled like old cigarettes and turpentine, though. In the shadows, I could hear clicking and popping. The roaches were watching us, maybe even waiting to swarm us.

There was a door open ahead of us; light spilled from it.

I heard singing. As we walked in, what I saw sent my heart up to my throat and down to my feet.

My mother was tied to a chair in the corner of the room. Her eyes widened when she saw us. She looked exhausted and terrified, and all I wanted to do was race to her. Standing in the center of the room was Mueller, bouncing my little sister in his arms as he sang her a German lullaby. The smile on his face grew as he saw me walk in. It was sinister and sharp, like it was carved into his face. Above them were dozens of the same balloons as upstairs. Now I knew where the turpentine smell came from. He'd filled the balloons with flammable liquid, even doused the hallways. There was a book of matches in his left hand.

Maybe I was wrong. Maybe his anger had finally pushed him past the fear, and now with all of us present, he was more than prepared to burn it all down on top of us. There was something in Mueller's eyes, something manic, something desperate. This was who he truly was, the man once again at his wit's end in the basement of a building he wanted to burn. No rhyme, no reason. Just fury and hate.

"Manuel, I am so glad you have come to join us." He placed Gracie down, and a collection of the biggest roaches I'd ever seen congregated around her. They stayed still, waiting for me to make the wrong move.

Mueller opened the book of matches and smiled wildly. "I am so happy everyone is finally here," he said.

CHAPTER 30

"THIS DOESN'T HAVE TO HAPPEN LIKE THIS, please. Please, let them go," I said. "Sasha can take them upstairs, and then you can have me. I'm the one who ruined everything for you, right? Take it out on me, not them."

Mueller stared at me. "Look at you," he said. "It's as if you've grown taller since the last time I saw you. Such a man with his puffed-out chest. Your people call that 'machismo,' yes?"

I held my palm toward him. "Mueller, I'm not playing this game anymore. Let them go, and you get me."

"What? No." My mother struggled against her bonds. "Al, don't you dare let him."

Al looked at me. He didn't speak but locked his eyes on mine. An acknowledgment of trust.

I took a step forward. "If you want me to burn this place down for you, I will. If you want to do it yourself, knowing that you got revenge on me, I'll stay. All this craziness that led us here, maybe it would have been better if this was what you did at first, but that's whatever at this point. All you have to do is let my family and my friend leave here, and you'll get what you want."

Mueller frowned. "I was hoping you'd do more than that, Manuel. I was hoping you would fight." He turned to my mother. "Do you know how strong your boy is? What I did to him had already killed two dozen people." Mueller turned back to me. "But you. You survived. Maybe it's your youth. I wager it was all that anger." He laughed. "Whatever it was, it helped me realize then that an empty building wasn't what I wanted. Perhaps what I wanted was to be surrounded by youth like you, Manuel. Strong-willed, angry . . . pliable." The smile on his face held no joy.

"Oh my god, someone shut this dude up," Sasha said.

Mueller looked at her with an almost manic glee. "It's those like you and the very idea of another home being sullied once again that have brought us here. Your 'affordable units'—I couldn't abide it. That was when I realized I had to purify this place again, that no matter what I did, the wrong element would return repeatedly unless I went to an extreme."

I held my hand up to stop Sasha as soon as I saw her tense. Mueller sure was a racist piece of crap, but he was also dangerous as all hell, and there was a baby in the room.

"Even with everything you've done, I don't think you're so far gone you'd hurt a child," I said.

Mueller laughed. "Then you are still naive."

Al made a stupid move. He rushed Mueller and practically emailed the punch he was going to swing. Mueller didn't move out of the way. Rather, he held his ground, and his hand was on Al's throat before I could even register movement. He lifted Al, a man twice his weight, into the air with ease.

"I am tired of this." Mueller casually tossed Al to the side. Al crashed to the ground, and I heard a loud snap. He screamed and rolled onto his back, holding his left leg; his foot pointed in the wrong direction.

Shit.

Mueller turned to us, a vicious grin on his face. "And you two, what will you do now? Who will you risk? The mother or the child? How much more fun can we have before the end, eh?"

The roaches surrounding Gracie began to crawl on her. She whimpered in fear and looked at my mother. My mother's eyes widened, and tears fell down her face. There was no talking this out. Mueller *was* too far gone.

Sasha, thankfully, read my mind. She held up her hand— she was holding a roach bomb—and indicated my mask. I nodded.

"Everyone, hold your breath!" I cried just before slipping my mask back on.

Sasha set off the bomb and threw it at Mueller, who flinched and moved away long enough for her to sprint forward and scoop Gracie into her arms. She covered Gracie's face and raced for the exit.

"Manny!" she called out as she threw something in my direction.

I caught the small object. It was a knife. I ran to my mother, unsheathing the blade and quickly moving to cut her bonds.

"Go with Sasha and Gracie. Get the hell out of here," I said.

Mom gave me a look.

"Ma, get out of here, now!"

Mom listened and rushed out of the room. All that was left was Al. I looked over, and he had his shirt over his mouth and was dragging himself toward the exit. I stepped between him and Mueller. The old man seemed only slightly affected by the roach bomb; he was twitchy, as if something inside him was reacting to the poison.

Sasha ran back into the room and joined me at my side.

"I told you to get the hell out of here," I said.

"Your mother and the baby got to the stairs safe," Sasha said as she squared up. "You honestly thought I was going to leave you two down here?"

Mueller raised a hand. "Peter, komm her." His voice was raspy, weak.

From the shadows, Peter appeared and grabbed Sasha violently. He was clearly possessed. His skin was split all over, the wounds bleeding and alive with roaches. Easily lifting Sasha off her feet, he joined his grandfather, holding a wounded hand over her mouth, the roaches in his skin skittering out and crawling onto her face.

My mouth went dry. "Peter," I said. "If you can hear me, fight this."

Mueller snorted. "Ah, please. He is gone. At least like this, he is no longer a disappointment."

I moved to help Sasha, but Mueller stepped in my way and charged at me. He tackled me to the ground, knocking the wind out of me, and straddled my chest. His hands were around my throat in the blink of an eye, and he cackled wildly as he leered.

"If we will not burn together, then you will do my bidding," he croaked as he tightened his grip. "As will your little girlfriend."

Mueller opened his mouth, and roaches poured out onto my face and into my hair. He took his hands from my neck and attempted to remove my mask. I swatted at the roaches, desperate to keep my mask on—if he was able to possess me again, that would truly be the end.

As we struggled, I felt a sting in my lower back.

The knife.

Was Mueller susceptible to a knife? Did it matter? It was what I had. I gave up my leverage to get a hand behind me and pulled the knife from beneath me. I thrust it into Mueller's midsection as hard as I could. He looked down, startled to see the blade protruding from his chest, and I took the opportunity to drag the knife down from his sternum to his stomach. I pulled the knife out, and it made this weird little *pop* sound.

Mueller sat up and stumbled back, which allowed me to get away from him. He poked a finger into the gash I'd made, and a collection of roaches poured out. I could see his flesh under his overalls; it was gray and curdled. Like rotted meat.

Sasha somehow managed to escape Peter's grip and rushed forward, delivering a kick to the same area I'd stabbed. Mueller let out a yelp and rolled farther away from us as more roaches escaped through the wound. He struggled to pull himself up into a crawl. Sasha helped me onto my feet.

"What did I tell you about knives?" she said.

"You were totally right."

"Scheiße." Mueller spat on the floor and pointed at us. "A knife. Just like that little savage friend of yours to teach you to use a weapon."

I was so tired of his bullshit pontificating. I passed the knife over to my right hand and held it out. "You can still stop this."

Mueller held his midsection and snarled. "Stop my work?" He rose to his knees and held his arms out. Thick brown liquid gummed the edges of his wound as roaches continued to pour out. They scrambled around Mueller's chest and up his arms, crawling into his gaping mouth. The smell of rotting fruit was strong and sharp. It burned my eyes and clung to the inside of my mouth.

I shook my head. "I wasn't talking to you, shithead."

The click of a lighter made Mueller turn. Peter was holding one of the balloons. He stared at his grandfather, anger and pain in his faded eyes, and threw the balloon directly at the old man. It burst, dousing Mueller in liquid. And then Peter tossed the lit lighter at his grandfather. Flame instantly blossomed from Mueller's center, engulfing him. The fire stretched up to the ceiling, and the first of the balloons popped, raining fire down to the floor.

I quickly ran to Al and pulled him up, taking care to keep his broken foot off the ground. Sasha went to the other side and provided support. We had to get the hell out of there as soon as we could, before we went up in flames next.

CHAPTER 31

THE SMOKE FOLLOWED US, THICK AND acrid. It nearly blinded me.

"The fire's catching up . . . ," Al yelped as I tripped on a step.

"Sorry, sorry." I readjusted Al's weight and looked at Sasha. "You got him?"

"I got him. Keep moving," she said.

We were close to the top of the final flight of stairs leading back into Blackrock Glen's boiler room. Smoke billowed around us. Even though there weren't more balloons above us, the smell of turpentine was thick. Mueller must have drenched the stairs and walls in it, hoping the fire would scale the stairs and breach Blackrock Glen's basement, where he'd set up more balloons.

I swore I heard screams behind us but chose to ignore them. Let Mueller and Peter work that out between themselves. My arms and legs were shaking, Al's weight and the slow rush up the stairs doing us no favors. I started coughing. Just that tickle cough at first, but it was beginning to hit my chest. Sasha and I were lucky to have masks, but I could only imagine how much Al was struggling. The fire was catching up with us. Whether I could see it or not, it didn't matter. If we didn't get out of this building, we were going to die.

We made our way through the basement at Blackrock Glen to Stairwell A, the very same stairs I'd come down while looking for mops on the fateful night I'd met Mueller. Behind us, I heard the first pop—the fire had reached the boiler room. The basement would soon turn into an oven, and once the liquid in those balloons ignited, the whole building was going up.

Sasha took my phone and texted my mother as I helped Al get up the stairs.

"She's outside with the baby and has called the fire department—they're on their way," Sasha said.

Awesome. They were safe. As soon as we could get outside, this would be over. I wouldn't have to worry about my family, and that rat-bastard piece of trash could burn up with the rest of Blackrock Glen.

We reached the entrance, and I rushed forward to open

the first of the two doors. Sasha led Al through it.

We were steps from fresh air. There were sirens in the distance.

But when I moved to get the next door for Sasha and Al, my feet left the ground, and I was pulled back through the shattering glass of the interior vestibule door. I was in the air long enough to twist my body around and see the charred and incredibly angry face of Gerhard Mueller as he roared.

"Ich bringe dich um!" Mueller threw me against the far wall.

I struggled to breathe, my chest spasming and the pain running from my throat down to my stomach. I wanted to vomit and cough at the same time, but the lack of air wouldn't let either happen. I lay on my side and, remembering I still had Sasha's knife, fished it out of my back pocket as I blinked through a sudden rush of tears.

Mueller stood and picked me back up. "I would have helped you," he muttered. "Made you the man you were meant to be." He pressed me against the wall and wrapped his hands around my throat again. "You offered to burn with me before. Now you will get your way." Mueller laughed. "They will watch us burn."

I found the strength to lift my arm and swing the knife in a wide arc. I caught Mueller on the cheek, and the skin split open. He wasn't like the possessed—there was meat there. No blood, but still substance. Roaches crawled through the new opening. They were massive—fat and black with thick, barbed legs.

Mueller screamed, spittle flying from his mouth and onto my face. The roaches fell to the ground at our feet. His grip didn't loosen, so I kept swinging the knife, catching him on the face, arms, and chest. Each gash exposed thick, rheumy slime and grayed flesh. The smell of rotten meat mingled with the smoke in the air. Above us, I saw the little brown roaches that infested Blackrock Glen congregate, thousands upon thousands of them beginning to cover the ceiling, walls, and floor to watch Mueller kill me.

Sasha, once again, was suddenly by my side. She plunged a knife into Mueller's left arm and let out a warrior's scream. Mueller finally dropped me, and I gasped for air. He turned to Sasha, but she was ready with one of the roach bombs, which she set off and shoved deep into his screaming mouth. Mueller looked stunned and staggered back. I could see the bomb's smoke start to pour out of his various wounds. Mueller pulled the can from his mouth, a few of his teeth skittering to the ground, and threw it down the hallway. He scratched at his throat and growled. Some of the roaches that had been scrambling from his wounds fell to his feet, dead. Mueller stepped toward Sasha but stopped as he retched uncontrollably. His mouth opened, this time the edges tearing. From inside his mouth erupted the head of the largest roach I'd ever seen. It was bigger than my fist; its mandibles looked large and strong enough to crush bone. Its eyes were easily the size of mine. One antenna poked out from Mueller's mouth while the other burst through a nostril. All that hate and anger. It made him a perfect nest.

Sasha took my hand and pulled me toward the door. The hall was filled with smoke, and staring down to where we'd come from the basement, I saw the gentle flicker of flames. Shadows dancing against the far wall. The fire had spread, and we needed to get the hell out of there.

Mueller still had his own plan. He grabbed both of us and held tight. Sasha and I stabbed and slashed, but he wouldn't let go, and the roach crawling out of his face seemed just as enthused to get a piece of us as it tried to pull itself free from Mueller to snap at us with its mandibles.

"Oh my god, will you just fucking die again?!" Sasha yelled.

Behind Mueller, a burning figure appeared. It staggered toward us and grabbed Mueller from behind, pulling him off us. The figure smothered Mueller, and what remained of Mueller's body caught fire. The roaches falling from him burst into flame and were ashes before they touched the ground. The others who'd come out to watch the spectacle were soon scrambling to find an escape, the fire catching them faster than they could run, turning them into tiny embers for a split second. It was almost beautiful.

I grabbed Sasha's hand and pulled her away from the

scene, rushing to the exit and nearly crashing through the glass of the outer door. We both spilled out onto the sidewalk and turned to watch as the figure—Peter—dragged Mueller back toward the fiery depths of the basement. The fire finally spilled out from downstairs, enveloping them and the first floor as the flames licked upward.

Another set of hands grabbed me, and I turned around, ready to fight.

"You kids need to move," a firefighter said.

There were other first responders there, all staring aghast at the sight in front of them. Sasha and I were ushered to a safe distance across the street. I saw Mom and Gracie at the foot of an ambulance, where Al was being taken care of. Mom and I made eye contact, and she burst into tears, reaching her hands out to me. I started sobbing as I was put in the back of another ambulance. Two paramedics worked quickly to tend to me. I sat quietly as they did, watching the fire's glow beginning to intensify on every floor of the building.

CHAPTER 32

"YOU GOTTA STOP HUGGING ME SO HARD,"
I said as I pushed my mom away from me. Between the
smells and the need for oxygen, I couldn't bear having her
arms wrapped around me for another fifteen minutes.

They were treating Al in the ambulance next to mine. I
heard him complain about the EMTs cutting his pants, and
I laughed.

"Do you need me to tell them to get you anything?"
Mom asked. Gracie was asleep in her arms, a *Frozen* bandage
on her left arm, and that was it. All she needed was a bath.
"Are you comfortable?"

I shook my head. "No, Ma. Are *you* okay?"

Mom nodded sadly. "We'll talk about it another time."
She rubbed my arm. "You did good, Manny."

I slipped my oxygen mask back on. When an EMT passed, I raised my hand. "Hey, did she see anyone yet?" I pointed to my mother.

"Manny, I'm fine."

"Ma, get yourself checked. Gracie's going to need you, and it isn't like you can go back there." I motioned to Blackrock Glen, which was still burning. Another set of fire trucks was arriving at the far end of the block.

Mom stared at me, her eyes wet, and smiled tightly. She stroked my face with her hand and walked toward the EMT.

I closed my eyes and enjoyed the rush from the oxygen. Everything hurt, but the relief was worth it. For the first time in weeks, I felt . . . I didn't know what the right word was. Not relaxed.

It felt like I was home.

I felt a push against my side and opened my eyes.

Sasha waved to me with a smile. "Damn," she said. "I needed much less oxygen than you did."

"Please. I know you ditched them the minute they turned around."

Sasha laughed. "Maybe." She sat beside me. "Is your family doing all right?"

"Yeah." My throat was raw, and talking hurt. "Did you call your parents?"

"Oh, it's a mess," Sasha said. "They were in the city for dinner, but they're on their way here." She frowned. "If your mom and the baby need a place to go, I can ask."

"Mom will say she doesn't need the help, but we'd appreciate it." I held my hand up. "I reopened my stitches."

"Just blood this time, I hope."

"I was never happier to bleed in my life." I laughed, which made me cough, which hurt a lot.

Sasha crossed her arms and watched the busy street. "Can you believe we did this?"

I cleared my throat and winced. "Um, I think so? I have no idea how to process anything beyond the pain right now. The physical stuff is easy, but everything else feels impossible. How are we even talking in complete sentences and not screaming, you know?"

"At least people know about it."

"You think they'll believe it?"

"They saw it with their own eyes. I saw at least three cops recording Peter and Mueller burning."

I stared at Blackrock Glen. Multiple firefighters were using hoses to try to snuff out the fire, but it was already at the top floors. There was no stopping this. It almost felt right, though. That building had to go, or Mueller would never have gone away.

"You know, one of us should go to school for psychology and then fix the rest of us up," I said.

"Not for free, though."

"Absolutely not for free."

"How's Frankie?"

Sasha shook her head. "I tried calling his parents, but nobody picked up. I figure we can try to find him when we get to the hospital."

"Are you going? You seem like you're doing fine."

"Yeah," Sasha said. "I might not want to be stuck by myself in that ambulance, but I'm sure I breathed in what you did, and somebody's gotta keep an eye on you. As stupid as that sounds."

"Not stupid at all. We all need each other. I think that matters."

Sasha laughed. "Look at you. That smoke got you acting all peace and love."

The smoke did help the soft-boy feelings, but there was more to it than that. Even if Blackrock Glen became ashes, Mueller left all sorts of garbage behind. Physical and mental wounds. He scarred us, and if we ignored that, those wounds would only reopen. That's exactly what Mueller would have wanted.

"I'm sorry," I said.

"For what?"

"I didn't take you seriously at first. Maybe if I had, things would have been different. Maybe if I hadn't only started caring when it was about me, then we would have seen what Mueller was up to from the start." I raised a hand to stop the reply. "But I know the maybes aren't worth focusing on, and

I know there was a lot out of our control. I wanted to recognize where I messed up. I'll work to be better."

"You know what I'm going to say now, right?"

"I don't need to give you apologies. I need to do the work."

"Nailed it."

I stared at the sky. "Hey," I said. "A while back, you mentioned Hunter College, downtown."

"Yeah? What about it?"

"Why did you want to go there?"

"Social work. They're supposed to have a good program."

Huh. "That's helping people, right? Like, making sure that people without means get them?"

"Something like that. My aunt did it. She always warned me off because it was demanding. Still appealed to me."

"That's cool." I wondered if that was the right path for me.

"You're drifting off," Sasha said.

"A little," I answered.

Sasha stood and helped me lie down on the gurney and shifted me to the side so she could lie down beside me. "You mind if I rest with you?"

"That would be great," I answered.

I closed my eyes but didn't sleep. I listened to the noise around us, to the EMTs closing the back of the ambulance, felt the ambulance beginning to drive us to the hospital. I thought about my family and my future. I thought about my friend lying there with me and how thankful I was for everything she'd done.

I thought about how everything would be okay, so long as we worked to make it that way.

LATER

"THE THREE OF YOU, MOVE IN CLOSER," MY mother said as she angled her phone toward us. She motioned to Frankie. "To the left, sweetie—I only got half of you."

Sasha, Frankie, and I all posed, sweaty but happy, as our parents took way too many pictures on their phones—except for Sasha's dad, who had a Nikon with a huge lens. Frankie and I were in our graduation gowns, while Sasha was in a fancy dress. Her graduation had been the previous week, but she'd shown up to support us. I felt bad that she had to pull double duty on the pictures.

Gracie, having fought with my mom for a solid fifteen minutes to take pictures with us, finally broke off from one of my cousins and ran over. I scooped her up and gave her a raspberry.

"I'm hot," Sasha said through a smile. "Please stop taking pictures."

"The more you ask, the more they'll snap." I stuck my tongue out. Gracie joined me. Most of the parents frowned.

The pictures magically stopped after that. They'd be back at it during dinner, but we at least got a chance to get out of the sun. As we walked to the shade, I gave a few dozen handshakes and shared private jokes with some kids I had AP English with. One of them, Jason, reminded me about a show down in the Village on Saturday.

"You'll be there? My brother's band is playing at a dive bar nearby." Jason smacked my arm as he shook my hand.

"Definitely. My friend Clari is coming up from Texas. She's all about hitting up downtown and doing all the New York things, so you'll have to give me notes so I can pretend I went full local."

"Dude, you barely been here a year. It takes at least fifteen to be full local." Frankie smirked at me and then at Sasha. "And 'my friend Clari.' Oh please, you need to ask that girl out already."

I gently smacked Frankie's cap off his head.

Sasha sighed and picked up Frankie's cap. She wiped it off before putting it on his head and giving him a soft kiss on the lips. "You both driving with me to the restaurant?"

Frankie and I nodded. "Yeah. Where's your car?" I asked.

"I'm parked over by the factories on the other side of the trains."

Frankie grunted. "Damn. That's far."

"I wasn't about to pay for the meter, and it's only, like, three blocks away," Sasha said.

Frankie lifted his gown and stuck his hands in his pants pockets. "Yeah. Gimme twenty minutes. I need to get some other pictures out of the way. My uncles are bitching that I'm eating dinner with my girlfriend instead of the family. Need to make it up to them."

I waved as the two of them walked away. "Enjoy."

I slipped off my own cap and opened the leather binder with my diploma. I smiled. I'd earned this, hadn't I?

"You know you can get a decent job with only that diploma, right? No need to go into a million years of debt at a liberal arts college or whatever." Al sidled by me with a grin. He switched his cane to his good side and leaned against me. "You feeling good?"

I nodded. "Yeah. Kind of a crazy year."

"You can say that again."

We laughed.

Al cleared his throat. "I'm proud of you—you know that, right?"

"I do. I do." I pointed to the cane. "Proud of you, too. Mom's been yelling for you to use that thing for a while now."

Al shrugged. "Yeah, well, it looks good with the suit."

"Absolutely."

"It makes me look like a very important man, you know?"

"Oh, you think? I figured it was more of a low-rent pimp kind of thing. Though it works, you know?"

We laughed again.

Al shook his head and turned to me. He took my face in his hands and gave me a gentle slap on the back of the head. "I can't wait to see what you do." He pulled me into a hug and patted my back. "Love ya, kid."

I hugged Al back. "Love you, too, Dad."

"We'll see you at the restaurant?" He took a few steps away from me and leaned on his cane.

"Yeah, I'm coming in with Sasha and Frankie."

"Good," Al said. "See you there." He walked off to my mom and Gracie.

Alone again, I took off my cap and gown. I stared at the people celebrating and smiled at the other students. It was hot—this humidity was still a killer—but it was a beautiful day. All that celebrating. All those futures coming together. It felt good. Like home.

Something caught my eye on the ground. At first I thought it was a leaf blowing in the breeze, but looking over, I saw a fat water bug on its back. Dark and ugly. Little black legs scrambling and antennae twitching. It rocked back and forth, trying to get right side up. I walked over and edged my foot toward it enough to give it a little boost to get back on its feet. The roach frantically fled into a crack in the pavement.

Not a terrible day to be a survivor, I thought.

ACKNOWLEDGMENTS

There's a Catholic school on Castle Hill Avenue in the Bronx—not far from where this story takes place—where an English teacher gave an eleven-year-old the insane idea he could write. Thank you, Mr. Grome. Turns out you weren't far off the mark.

Thank you to my agent, Jon Michael Darga, and editor, Christian Trimmer. From a random conversation in a bar to a full-fledged novel; if it wasn't for your guidance and cheerleading, this book would be nowhere near as fully realized on the page as it was in my head. I am deeply grateful for the faith placed in me and for the opportunity to write a story I would have killed to read when I was younger.

To Nik Korpon, Chris Irvin, Chris Holm, Hector Acosta, and Shawn Cosby—thank you for being more of a part of this process than any of you realize. Just having folks to vent to and share good news with kept me moving forward.

To other Puerto Rican writers, like Ernesto Quiñonez, Xochitl Gonzalez, Jaquíra Diaz, Richie Narvaez, Amparo Ortiz, Elena Aponte, and Cina Pelayo—thank you for being sources of inspiration and a reminder that our stories deserve to be told.

And thank you to Jeanette. I don't know what I did to deserve a partner like you, but I am so very thankful for your support and love.

ABOUT THE AUTHOR

Angel Luis Colón is a Derringer Award– and Anthony Award–nominated author, whose works include *Hell Chose Me*, the Blacky Jaguar series of novellas, *No Happy Endings*, and the short story collection *Meat City on Fire and Other Assorted Debacles*. His fiction has appeared in multiple web and print publications, including *Thuglit*, *Literary Orphans*, and *Great Jones Street*. *Infested* is his debut YA novel. For more information, visit AngelLuisColon.com.